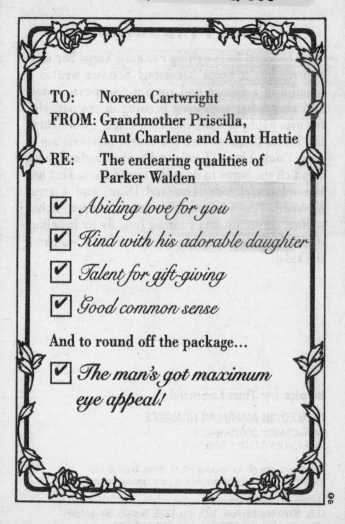

TO: Noreen Cartwright

FROM: Grandmother Priscilla,
Aunt Charlene and Aunt Hattie

RE: The endearing qualities of
Parker Walden

☑ *Abiding love for you*

☑ *Kind with his adorable daughter*

☑ *Talent for gift-giving*

☑ *Good common sense*

And to round off the package...

☑ *The man's got maximum
eye appeal!*

ABOUT THE AUTHOR

Tina Leonard feels writing romance keeps her sane and reading it keeps her going! She has written a handful of romance and romantic suspense novels and always has something brewing in the pot. Her favorite hobby is traveling, even if it's just watching the Travel Channel! Her two dream vacations are to drive Route 1 in California and to visit England, both of which she hopes to do in the near future. Tina has two wonderful kids, Lisa and Dean, and a great husband, Tim, who was instrumental in getting her writing career up and running (mainly by installing usable software on her computer and watching the kids)!

Books by Tina Leonard

HARLEQUIN AMERICAN ROMANCE

The Most Eligible...Daddy

TINA LEONARD

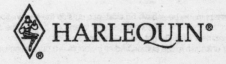

HARLEQUIN®

TORONTO • NEW YORK • LONDON
AMSTERDAM • PARIS • SYDNEY • HAMBURG
STOCKHOLM • ATHENS • TOKYO • MILAN • MADRID
PRAGUE • WARSAW • BUDAPEST • AUCKLAND

ISBN 0-373-16771-7

THE MOST ELIGIBLE...DADDY

Chapter One

"Is it my imagination or did the scenery just improve drastically?" Hattie Mayes asked, perking up from perusing the Sunday-afternoon strollers meandering around the town square in Rockwall, Texas.

Her two sisters, whom she sat between, gave her a thorough eyeing.

"Certainly it's good fall weather for Texas, Hattie," Priscilla Cartwright replied. Her eyes, still alert at seventy, stared piercingly at her youngest sister as if Hattie had suddenly become more interesting than she had been a moment ago. "Nothing we haven't seen before, right, Charlene?"

"Right as always, Priscilla," Charlene Starling agreed, in a voice that said to suggest otherwise would be useless.

"No, you gooses!" Hattie whispered in her best stage whisper, though no one else could hear their conversation. "Look by the water fountain!"

All three women looked toward the water fountain situated in the center of the square in front of the old courthouse.

"Well, we've said many times over that Bert Lester

did a wonderful job designing that fountain,'' Priscilla began.

"Check out the man!'' Hattie interrupted, realizing this could go on forever if she didn't cut to the chase. "The man standing over there, with his little girl.''

"Most definitely a man we've never seen before,'' Charlene mused.

"*Now* we're getting somewhere.'' Hattie sighed and leaned back against the park bench.

The three women stared in appreciation for a moment. "I don't know about you, but that's the kind of man I always wanted to fill my dance card,'' Charlene said dreamily.

"Okay, so we've established he's dance card material,'' Priscilla said drily. "What do we do with that piece of trivia?''

The women stared at Hattie expectantly.

"Don't you have a granddaughter still sitting on the shelf, Priscilla? My goddaughter?''

It was a sore point with Priscilla, though she suspected the goddaughter in question, Noreen Cartwright, wouldn't appreciate the inquiry, either. Noreen was fabulously beautiful, smart enough to attend Stanford and graduate summa cum laude and independent enough to set firecrackers under the saddle of any man who tried to make easy time with her. Noreen had returned to Rockwall after college to take over the family farm. She didn't have time to sit and admire water fountains.

Or fabulous-looking men.

"Noreen may be on the shelf,'' Priscilla replied haughtily, "but it's by her own choosing.''

"Hmmph.'' Hattie knew all about shelf sitting. All that was going to get Noreen was a lonely spot on a wooden bench like they were occupying. "I say you best get over there and introduce yourself, Priscilla."

"Introduce myself! He has a child with him, Hattie Mayes! Are you saying that Noreen should stoop to having an affair with a married man because no eligible bachelor wants her?"

Hattie sighed, beleaguered. "He's a single father."

"Really?" Priscilla and Charlene chorused, sitting up and peering at the man who was helping his little girl, who looked about four, balance on the side of the fountain. "How can you tell?"

"It's Sunday afternoon. There is no mother in sight. Those two factors lead me to believe that he's having visitation with his child."

"That's the most flawed piece of logic—"

Hattie waved Priscilla quiet. "If you don't at least go over there and introduce yourself, somebody else is going to strike up a conversation with him, and Noreen is going to lose out on prime boy toy material."

"Boy toy?" Priscilla and Charlene repeated, heads snapping around to stare at Hattie.

She preened under their astonishment. "That's a boy toy if I ever saw one." Her delight at showing off her mod vocabulary faded immediately under their scrutiny. "What?"

"The only boy toy I ever saw was Madonna," Priscilla informed her, "and she was shamelessly advertising that on her belt buckle. So you've mixed your gender, and besides, do you see that man advertising that he wants attention of any kind?"

He did look rather content to be enjoying a warm afternoon with his adorably dressed little girl. Hattie felt a moment's guilt, but she would do anything for

Noreen, as any godmother worth her salt should. It was up to Hattie to see that the poor girl was removed from the shelf and thoroughly dusted off—the sooner the better.

"I'm going over there," she announced.

"You're doing no such thing." Her sisters reached out and put restraining hands on each of her arms. "Leave the man alone."

"Very well," Hattie replied, in such an innocent voice that she was believed, because the hands were removed. Hattie swept the courthouse with her gaze, before hurling her purse out into the middle of the street with all her might. "Help! Thief!" she cried loudly.

Apparently she still had cheerleader lungs because the man turned his head and looked their way. "Thief, thief!" Hattie wailed for good effect. Priscilla clapped a hand over Hattie's mouth, but Hattie pinwheeled her arms desperately. The man took his little girl down from the water fountain, tucking her against his hip as he crossed the street. Hattie slapped away the hand that was trying to keep her quiet and worked up a few tears.

"Are you all right, ma'am?" the stranger asked.

"I'm fine," she said in a quavering voice, pointing to her purse lying forlornly in the street. "Some young ruffian—"

"She's fine," Priscilla interrupted, pink-cheeked. "She's just having one of her paranoid delusions. There was no one—"

"Oh, oh!" Hattie wailed loudly. "He dropped my purse in the middle of the street and it's going to get run over!"

The man turned, spying the errant purse. Still keeping his daughter firmly in his arms, he headed into the street.

"Hattie!" Priscilla whispered stridently. "You're acting crazy!"

"You just hush and watch a pro in action," Hattie insisted. Smiling like an angel at her rescuer, she hissed the words out of the corner of her mouth at Priscilla.

"Here you go." Very carefully the man handed the purse to Hattie and knelt to gently stand his daughter beside him. Hattie could just feel the kindness in him. He was even more handsome than he'd been across the street. Distances could sometimes make her glasses play tricks on her eyes, but she hadn't been mistaken, thank heaven. Olivia Newton-John would risk no time in getting physical with this tall, dark-haired, hazel-eyed specimen.

"Are you all right?" he asked.

Priscilla broke out in sudden coughing, as if something had gotten caught in her throat, but she'd always been an attention grabber, Hattie thought sourly. She elbowed her sister and gave the stranger a piteous look. "Thank you," she said. "I'm fine. I didn't imagine that I would have to depend on the kindness of a stranger today. I'm so lucky you were in Rockwall visiting."

All the air went out of Charlene in some kind of histrionic sigh. Hattie was annoyed but didn't let the smile leave her face.

"We had heard this water fountain was worth seeing. It certainly is, isn't it, Meg?" he asked his daughter.

She beamed up at her daddy with an expression of sheer worship. Hattie's heart caught like a Sunday bonnet in a windstorm. This man was certainly worthy if his daughter adored him in such a manner. She resolved to be stalwart in her attempt to land this most eligible bachelor for Noreen.

"Do you have relatives in Rockwall, uh, Mr.—"

"Parker," he supplied.

"Mr. Parker, do you—"

He shook his head with a pleasant smile. "My name is Parker. Parker Walden."

"Oh, *Parker*," Hattie gushed. "Just like Parker Stevenson in the *Hardy Boys*—"

"I think you're laying it on a bit thick, Aunt Hattie."

Hattie's heart shriveled even as she turned to look in the doorway of the bakery behind them. Noreen Cartwright eyed her fondly, though a bit sternly. She held fresh flowers wrapped in florist paper and a white bag from the bakery, which boded well for dinner tonight. *Now if only I can finagle the dessert,* Hattie mused, her gaze immediately turning back toward Parker.

"Thick?" she repeated, wishing desperately that dear Noreen hadn't chosen this particular moment to show up. Things had been going so nicely! One could also wish that Noreen was wearing something more advantageous than those awful jeans. Too bad she'd changed after church! But Noreen's cooking would offset the tomboyish cowgirl impression Parker no doubt was receiving. After all, the way to a man's heart was through his finely toned stomach.

"Yes, a bit thick." Noreen leaned down and kissed her. "I heard the whole thing, Aunt Hattie." With surprising calm, she shuffled her packages and held out a hand to Parker. "Hi. I'm Noreen Cartwright.

I'm afraid you almost got caught in a matchmaking scam.''

"Really?" He looked mildly interested, and Hattie thought that was a good sign. "No thief?"

"No thief. Just a wonderful lady who used to play for a minor league girl's baseball team." Noreen looked down fondly. "Your pitching arm seems to be in good shape, if the distance you threw that purse is any indication, Aunt Hattie." She shared a conspiratorial smile with Parker. "Thank you for rescuing my athletic aunt, but please, we don't want to trouble you anymore. If you hurry, you can still see the art exhibit on the other side of the town square. It was nice to meet you," she told him. "I'll deal with *you* later," she said, placing a kiss on each woman's cheek.

And that was that, Hattie thought sadly, watching as her niece strode away. For heaven's sake, those long legs of hers made her walk rather like a man. If she'd just slow down, if she wasn't so businesslike, if she wouldn't wear those darn jeans, an eligible bachelor might be able to see the light Noreen was determined to hide under her bushel basket. *Noreen Cartwright Walden*, she mused. It sounded perfectly wonderful.

Parker was staring after Noreen, Hattie suddenly noticed, though she couldn't tell if that was a good sign. Had the two young people felt the spark, the instant flash of attraction required for courtship in this day and age?

She closed her eyes and wished for inspiration.

Next thing Hattie knew, Parker had gained his voice.

"Excuse me," he said to the ladies. "Hang on a

second!'' he called after Noreen, striding down the sidewalk with Meg in his arms.

"Oh, thank heaven!" Hattie exclaimed. She sank back against the bench, fairly worn out from her efforts. "He's got it all—looks, great bod, manners, and he's smart enough to know a good thing when he sees it."

"You're going to get yourself in trouble one day, Hattie Mayes," Charlene warned. "You're going to meddle one day and it's going to backfire."

"Charlene is certainly right. You're not the fairy godmother you think you are," Priscilla informed her huffily. "You'd better be careful where you aim your knitting needles."

"Oh, hush, both of you. You're just mad because I'm faster on my feet than either of you. Always have been. Always will be." She stared down the street at the couple, greatly satisfied with her results.

She'd provided the introduction and the opportunity to Noreen, as any decent, dutiful godmother would. But only so much could rest in her capable hands. The rest was up to Noreen.

Unfortunately, her goddaughter was about as interested in suitors as a cat was in getting a bath.

Chapter Two

Parker strode toward the blonde in jeans as if an unseen hand was planted in the middle of his back propelling him toward her. He had no idea what he was going to say.

All he knew was that he couldn't let her just walk away.

"Yes?" Noreen asked as he and Meg reached her side.

Her smile was friendly, but cool. Questioning. Definitely not welcoming. Parker swallowed down a slight attack of masculine concern that she didn't seem interested in him. What the heck was he going to say to her?

"Hi!" Meg said, her cherubic voice filling the silence.

"Hello, sweetheart." Noreen's eyes softened as she looked down at the little girl.

Parker's heart swelled with pride as he, too, glanced at Meg. Her cute Sunday dress showed off chubby little legs. She had dark hair, like his. He'd awkwardly put a green barrette at the top of her head to try to keep the long wavy strands out of her face, without success.

"She's pwetty, Daddy."

"I know." The back of his neck warmed under the sun's bright rays, but that warmth had more to do with the fact that he found Noreen astonishingly attractive than with the day's heat. So that he wouldn't have to meet Noreen's eyes, he made himself busy placing Meg on the sidewalk beside him. His perceptive child and her wonderful honesty had put him on the spot! "Miss Noreen is very pretty."

"Thank you." Noreen's gaze caught on Parker's for only a second before she glanced back to Meg. Her smile to the little girl was genuine as she squatted to meet her at eye level. "Has anybody ever told you that you're very pretty, too?"

"Daddy does," Meg said with confidence. "A lot. He says he likes pwetty things, and I'm a pwetty thing."

"I see." Noreen stood, her light, expressive brows raised slightly.

"Like water fountains," Parker hastened to insert, lest Noreen think he was hitting on her because she was pretty. There was something more about this woman than mere beauty. The loving way she'd handled her meddling family was part of it. He glanced back at the bench, seeing three little gray-headed ladies craning at them with great interest. "We came out to see the water fountain and Rockwall's town square. And a few other sights."

This nonconversation had to go someplace. He had called out to Noreen for a reason. As uncomfortable as it was, he had to put his rusty dating technique to work and be honest about what he wanted from Noreen. Her phone number, maybe. A chance to see her again. Something told him she was worth getting to know better.

"I'm thirsty, Daddy," Meg suddenly complained. "And I'm hot."

Uh-oh. He heard the crankiness. It was nearing two o'clock, and Meg's nap time. Looking with regret at Noreen, he knew he couldn't just blurt out some ill-formed pick-up line his frat buddies had tossed around in college like, *I seem to have forgotten my phone number. Can I borrow yours?*

"Well—" he began.

"There's a soda shop across the street," Noreen said at the same time.

He perked up considerably. "Oh?" Making a big show of glancing over his shoulder, he acted as if he were seeing the shop for the first time. He'd checked out the town square immediately upon arrival, his eye for commercial real estate always searching for new possibilities, so why not say so?

Maybe because it was the first time since his ex-wife had packed up and left him for a freer, Bohemian lifestyle that he'd found himself incredibly, strongly interested in a woman. Expressing some casual interest shouldn't be as hard as it felt, he reminded himself sternly.

Now it was Noreen who appeared ill-at-ease. "Maybe your daughter would like a root beer," she said hurriedly. "Or some ice cream."

"Yes! Oh, Daddy! Please?" Meg hopped up and down like a cricket beside him.

Ah, Noreen had done that neatly. A well-thrown hint and then the ball back in his court. "Can I buy you one, too, Noreen?"

Their gazes met and held for a second that communicated awareness—and some curiosity—on both sides. Parker held his breath.

"Sure. Let me put this bread in my truck. You go on ahead so Meg can cool off, and I'll meet you inside."

He nodded. "See you in a minute."

Meg grabbed his hand and dragged him toward the shop, delighted that she was going to get a treat. The truth was, he was feeling a little excited himself— something he hadn't felt in a long time.

NOREEN TOLD HER HEART to stop pounding so hard. She was simply being nice to a man whose daughter was hot and tired! It wouldn't take more than thirty minutes. She wasn't doing it because she felt anything for him, or his delightful little Meg.

Idly, she wondered about the girl's mother. *It doesn't matter,* she told herself firmly. *This isn't a date.*

But it was the first time she'd agreed to go out with a man whom she hadn't known since she was in elementary school. Even at college, she'd gone out only if a large group of friends were heading out together. The relationship process, where one had to let the seeds of trust bud and grow, had never made her comfortable. It wasn't exactly that she didn't trust men, even though her younger stepbrother, Garrison, could make the most trusting soul suspicious—a fact she hated to admit. But at twenty-eight, Noreen found it best to rely mostly upon herself.

Peeking over her shoulder as she put the sacks into her truck, Noreen watched as the big, dark-haired man helped his tiny child walk inside the restaurant. Parker seemed so handsome in a good way, and so nice...but blond, lanky Garrison had that same effect on anyone he met, too. She was well aware that appearances could be deceiving: a charming package of good looks and excellent manners didn't always translate to honor and integrity in a man.

In fact, charming could be downright disastrous.

Yet, in spite of the dire warning her mind issued, Noreen took a deep breath and closed the truck door, turning toward the restaurant. Surely thirty minutes with Parker wouldn't hurt a thing.

GARRISON COULDN'T believe his eyes when he saw his stepsister join the man and his daughter in a booth in the back of the Good Times Soda Shop and Diner. He didn't know the man, and it surprised him that Noreen had a lunch date. She never went out with anyone, preferring to spend all her time at her run-down farm with her three unbalanced relatives.

He couldn't stand the ranch, himself. All that dirt made him feel like he could never get the grit out of his teeth. The smell of horses and manure disgusted him. Last week, he'd accidentally driven his Ferrari over a cow patty, ruining the Armor All shine on the tire and bursting an odoriferous cloud over his day. If he never heard the sounds of the country again, he would die happy. Moreover, the day he got out of this squatty little town for good, he intended to celebrate in grand style. Every day of his life he literally hungered to leave the ranch. Selling his forty-four percent of Cinderella Acres would bring tears to his eyes—tears of joy, for being able to finally live in the manner he enjoyed. His stepfamily had stood in his way too long. From the day his mother had married Noreen's father and brought him to live on the farm, his five-year-old wisdom had told him that he would never, ever be a real part of this family or their stinking, country lifestyle.

His gaze narrowed on Noreen as she shyly glanced at her lunch date. Was that interest he saw sparkling in her too-demure gaze?

"What else can I get ya, Garrison?" the waitress asked.

"Nothing." He waved her off without even looking up. His interest was entirely caught by the scenario in the booth across the restaurant, and he didn't want Noreen spotting him until he'd had a chance to figure out what she was up to. She had never mentioned a man to him. And suddenly he wondered why she would bother to be so secretive—unless she was planning something.

His mind ticked as he ran through the possibilities. If she liked this man, and his little girl, who from the look of things, certainly appeared to have taken a liking to Noreen, a marriage could, as inconceivable as it seemed, occur. He'd never had to worry about Noreen marrying before. She was as prickly around men as a cactus, and that suited Garrison just fine. Being the only man on a ranch with females meant he could be the powerbroker, never mind that Noreen seemed to think it was she, with all her independent airs. No, he ran the show as he saw fit, always allowing Noreen to think she was the boss.

But another man...that might cause a problem.

He'd better see what was going on. Garrison put money down for his tab and headed over to Noreen's booth.

"Howdy, Sis," he said blithely, his eyes taking the measure of Noreen's companion.

"Hi," Noreen said, her tone surprised and reluctant. "Parker, this is my brother, Garrison. Garrison, this is Parker Walden, and his daughter, Meg. They're visiting from Dallas."

"Dallas," Garrison said congenially, shaking Parker's hand in a grip he purposely made firm to communicate his strength. "What brings you here?" He took a seat next to Noreen though she hadn't invited him.

"I was looking at some properties." Parker shifted his gaze from Garrison to Noreen, assessing their reaction. "I had heard there was acreage for sale out this way, and I've got clients looking to expand their concerns. Rockwall seems to be an area with great future growth potential."

Garrison perked up, though he felt Noreen stiffen beside him. "You don't say? We could use some corporate growth in Rockwall, couldn't we, Noreen? Lessen the tax burden on the citizens if some companies are paying for it."

"Yes," she agreed slowly.

Garrison knew he had her with that one. Noreen loved Rockwall, and growth was good for the town. Of course, getting her to sell that blasted run-down farm she called Cinderella Acres would be his dream come true, but if he played his cards right, those batty relatives of hers might be living in a nursing home yet.

He eyed Parker thoughtfully. The stranger could be a golden chance to get him out of the financial straits he found himself in, which were getting deeper all the time.

The only thing standing in his way was Noreen. She was determined not to sell even a square inch of her grungy little queendom, though it was basically falling apart at the seams. If she broke even this year, it would be a miracle direct from Heaven. It just killed Garrison that his money was tied up in a losing venture.

But he wasn't going to play Noreen's humble servant forever. Fortunately, Garrison ruminated with a sly, private smile, he had a few trumps he could play if necessary—named Hattie, Charlene and Priscilla. His stepsister would do everything within her power to assure the well-being of her tottering grandmother and aunts. It suddenly occurred to him that a real estate developer who was already on her good side stood a much better chance of purchasing land than one who cold-called. Noreen would get the old ladies to gang up on anyone Garrison suggested, but Parker, from the look of things, was already working his way into her hard-to-win trust.

"You know, Parker," he said casually, as if he issued heartfelt invitations every day, "you and Meg should swing by the house on your way out of town. Noreen serves decent fried chicken on Sunday nights, and your little girl might enjoy riding a pony."

Noreen's eyes lit with instant suspicion and panic. Parker didn't see because he was wiping some ice cream from his daughter's chin with a napkin.

"Can we, Daddy? Can we?" Meg's hopeful eyes turned pleading on her father.

Garrison smiled to himself, assessing the degree of effectiveness his bombshell invitation was having on both Parker and Noreen. Ah, those two were trying to play it so cool, but by their cautious glances at each other, there was more than a simple conversation over ice cream going on.

"Yes," Noreen seconded, her voice only a trifle hesitant, "Why don't you join us for dinner?"

"Well," Parker hedged, his eyes on Noreen, "If you really don't mind last-minute guests, I suppose it would be all right."

No one at the table moved for what Garrison calculated was a long five seconds. Then Noreen's manners rescued the situation.

"Of course not." Her voice held warmth and enthusiasm. "I should have thought of inviting you out myself. Garrison has always been better at the social amenities than I have." She sent her brother a slight smile. "And those three ladies who had you running around after handbags earlier will be thrilled for the company." Noreen rose to her feet, putting her hand out to little Meg, who accepted it eagerly. "Would you like to ride in my truck, sweetie?"

"Yes!" Meg followed Noreen out of the booth. "And can I really ride a pony?"

"Yes. If your father says it's okay." A nod from Parker assured her it was. "After the sun goes down a little tonight, so that it's not too hot for the horses," Noreen told her with an innocent look Garrison's way, "my brother will be more than happy to take you riding for as long as you like. Right, Garrison?"

He stiffened instantly at the repulsive twin realizations that his stepsister had neatly foxed him not only into being around a beast he despised, but also with a small child in tow. Children and horses were two things he avoided strenuously. But he couldn't back out of his own invitation.

"Wouldn't miss it for the world," he said with a false smile.

The four of them walked out into the baking-hot

sunshine, but that heat was nothing compared to the burning of Garrison's eyes as he watched Noreen help Meg into her truck. Parker slid in beside the two of them.

It was all so cozy. Everything always was with Noreen. She could charm plumed birds out of scrub trees and healthy plants out of sun-cooked soil. She was the lucky one, with the good heart of an angel.

If I have my way, Garrison vowed, waving congenially as Noreen's truck pulled past, *her luck is about to change—for the worse.*

Chapter Three

The red truck, which had seen more than its share of produce hauls to market, bounced over the uneven farm road to Cinderella Acres. Noreen glanced over Meg's head at her newly acquired guest as she drove. "If I'd known you were interested in Rockwall real estate, I would have suggested you come out this way, Parker." It was a wonderful excuse to spend more time with this man without having to put more than a casual face on it.

"Why? Do you have land you're looking to sell?" Parker's gaze was curious.

"Oh, no." Noreen would never sell a piece of her beloved ranch. "It's just that we have a neighbor behind us who wants to move closer to her family. We'll drive past it before we get to mine."

"You're not in the market to add to your own place?"

She shook her head. "No. I've got all I can handle. Garrison isn't cut out for farming, so I do most of the work. I don't mean to make it sound like he doesn't help out," she said hurriedly. "It's just that farming's my love, not his."

"I see. What does Garrison do?"

"Well..." Noreen thought that over swiftly. "He spends a lot of time in Dallas, but to be honest, I've never really known what he does. He's always been very private about his life."

Parker didn't comment, and suddenly Noreen realized that she might have given the impression that she and her stepbrother weren't close. They really weren't, Noreen realized with a pang, but that wasn't something she'd been prepared to admit to herself until now. She certainly didn't want Parker thinking ill of her family. Since her father had died, Noreen had worked hard to hang on to the farm. If Garrison didn't share her love of hard work and crop producing, she was willing to overlook that. They were family, and it was her duty to accept him as he was. It was what her father had wanted during his lifetime: a family that took care of each other and loved each other as true-blood relations.

"Do you have lots of ponies?" Meg asked in a wondering tone.

"A few." Noreen smiled down at the dark-haired girl beside her. She was a gorgeous child, with Parker's eyes in a delicate face. Obviously Meg's mother was lovely and petite, she thought with a small pang that felt strangely like wistfulness for her own rather tomboyish physique. Quickly Noreen pulled her gaze back to the road. *I'm a farmer.* She reprimanded herself for her sudden attack of vanity. She lived outdoors; she needed to be fit for the kind of work she did. If she'd been a delicate woman, she might never have been able to do as much on her struggling farm as she did.

Still, the woman's heart she had so long denied

herself recognized instantly that she wanted Parker to
find her attractive.

"We have a few cows, too," she added to satisfy
Meg's curiosity and to cover the sudden awkward silence. She could feel Parker's gaze on her, and Noreen felt a sudden stinging of warmth in her cheeks.
"In fact, we have a Shetland named Meanie who will
be just right for you."

"Meanie?" Meg asked, her voice trembling.

"Meanie. The sweetest little pony you'd ever want
to ride on," she assured her. "You can even feed her
carrots. Would you like that?"

"Yes!" Meg's eyes were bright with excitement.
Noreen glanced up, at that moment catching Parker's
gaze on her. He had a soft smile on his well-defined
lips and something like gratitude in his large hazel
eyes, and suddenly Noreen knew, beyond a shadow
of a doubt, that she was more than attracted to the
handsome stranger from the city.

"DID YOU SEE THAT?" Hattie sat straight up on the
bench as Noreen drove past with a friendly wave.
"She had Parker and Meg in that truck with her!"

"I did see, Sister," Charlene replied, her voice reg-
istering her own surprise. "Perhaps you were right to
cause such a scene. It appears to have achieved de-
sirable results."

"We don't know that." Priscilla's tone, as always,
was superior and doubting. "The end result is what
will count, and we all know Hattie's results tend to
come out half-baked."

"Well, not this time." Hattie stood and straightened her dress. "I just have the best feeling in my

bones! You shouldn't be such an old sourpuss, Priscilla. It's bad for the lines around your mouth.''

"So is seeing Noreen get hurt by someone we know nothing about. Really, Hattie, you are far too impulsive. Just because the man is good-looking doesn't mean he'd treat our Noreen the way she deserves.'' Priscilla got to her feet alongside Hattie. "However, we should hurry home. We can at least help with the cooking tonight, and eject Noreen from the kitchen long enough for her to enjoy her gentleman caller.''

Hattie nodded and helped Charlene stand. "I'm glad to see you're willing to assist me on this project.''

"I'm willing to do anything for Noreen except meddle in her business too much. At your age it's time you quit, Sister.''

"Nonsense!'' Hattie's eyes were large and interested in her surroundings as they started off toward the local cab office. "I'm like fine wine, getting better with age. Besides, while Noreen's busy with Parker and his daughter, we can occupy Garrison.''

They all fell silent at that. As good, church-going women they all felt they shouldn't criticize out loud, but the unanimous opinion was that if their stepnephew had his way, they'd be rolling around in wheelchairs in a senior citizens' center.

"Don't think about it,'' Hattie said out loud to the ominous thought they were all thinking. "Let's first wheedle Ned Adams out of a free ride home. Then we'll plan how to keep Garrison busy tonight. After all,'' she said brightly, her face optimistic, "if we can get Noreen married, she'll have someone on her side. And that will water down Garrison's ability to manipulate Noreen's heart strings—and lessen our chance of going into an old folks' shelter, if he should ever manage to get the upper hand.''

"Isn't that rather selfish, though?" Charlene looked worried. "Aren't we using Noreen to fit our own wishes?"

"Yes," Hattie said, stepping into the cool interior of the cab office they haunted whenever possible for lifts around town. Ned was a longtime admirer of Hattie's and had been providing her with transportation service for years, not that it did him a whole lot of good. Hattie had once let him kiss her marshmallow-soft cheek, but that had been it. "Yes and no. Noreen needs a man, and we need to keep our independence. Parker may just be the key to our mutual satisfaction. Let's get home and see if we can keep Garrison from ruining our plans.''

PARKER CARRIED Meg in his arms as he followed Noreen inside a beautiful, white-painted brick farmhouse. His daughter had fallen asleep about the time they'd pulled up the pebbled drive. He decided to let her enjoy a nap. That way she wouldn't be fussy, and he'd get to spend some time alone with Noreen.

The woman made his mouth water. He had come out today hoping to scout the area for possibilities, but he'd never imagined he might meet a woman as beautiful, as seemingly kind, as Noreen Cartwright. It made him very grateful to her aunts for their apparent matchmaking attempt. He was enjoying an easy, no-strings-attached Sunday afternoon.

Noreen was tying an apron around her femininely curved frame. He supposed cooking was the next item on her agenda. "Can I help you?"

"No, thank you." She shook her head, glancing through to the small parlor where Parker had settled his child onto a small, overstuffed sofa. "You sit with Meg and take advantage of the air-conditioning. I'm going to heat this kitchen up by frying chicken. Can I get you a drink of something?"

"Water would be fine." He leaned against the counter, not about to abandon this prime opportunity to get to know Noreen better. She handed him a glass of ice-cold water with a shy glance. Parker felt breathless suddenly, like he'd been running a mile. "Thank you."

"You're welcome," she said softly, her eyes barely meeting his again.

She didn't seem to notice that her apron string was trailing in back, so Parker put the glass down and reached to turn her around to secure it. Her waist was so tiny, though she was a tall woman. His hands shook a bit, which bothered him. It had been a long time since he'd been this close to a woman. Noreen's fall of blond hair glistened under the kitchen lights, teasing with brilliance.

"There." He slowly turned her around again, his palms lingering on her shoulders. "All set."

Noreen didn't move and neither did he. A fan circled quietly overhead, but nothing else intruded on the suspended moment. *I'd like to kiss her,* Parker thought absently. *Just a small kiss.*

I wish he'd kiss me. Noreen stayed absolutely still, dreamy hope filling her. Never in her life had she wanted to be kissed so badly by a man, but this one had her swallowing in nervous anticipation.

And then, incredibly, his head bent toward hers. Sudden panic mixed with wonder filled her. She closed her eyes, waiting for the touch of his mouth against hers—

"Yoo-hoo!"

The front door slammed. Parker and Noreen each jumped a foot in opposite directions.

"Anybody home?" Hattie called. "We're here to help fry some chicken!"

"We're in here." Noreen sent a quick, embarrassed glance toward Parker. What bad timing her lovable relatives had! "Be real quiet, though, Aunt Hattie. Meg fell asleep on the way over."

"Oh, the poor dear." Hattie bustled into the kitchen, spying the flowers Noreen had bought and not yet put into a vase. She picked them up, preparing to remedy the situation. "Hello, Parker. You must be joining us for dinner."

"Yes." He gave Noreen a rueful smile.

"Good, good." Hattie jerked the careful bow Parker had tied on the back of Noreen's apron. "Give me that apron. You two go take a walk or something, and let Charlene and Priscilla help me cook dinner."

"Oh, no, I can—"

"Nonsense." The distressed glance Noreen sent Parker's way was completely missed by Hattie. "We'll cook, you entertain your guest." She beamed a delighted smile on Parker. "Charlene can keep an eye on your daughter. Have Noreen show you her prize pumpkin patch. It's going to be a bumper crop this year, I can just feel it in my bones."

"Okay." Parker stepped out of the kitchen behind a reluctant Noreen. "Do you think she's up to her same tricks?" he whispered mock-dramatically.

"Yes. I'm mortified." Noreen sent him a skittering glance. "I hope you're not offended by her obvious designs on you. I'm not looking for a relationship at all, though my grandmother's attempts at matchmaking may make you think otherwise.''

The fact that they had very nearly kissed obviously had her even more determined to make the point that she wasn't out to snare him. Parker hid a smile.

"Well, if it will make her happy to have you show me your pumpkins, let's do it.'' He crooked his brow. "Actually, I don't think that came out the way I meant it.''

"Never mind.'' Noreen laughed and pointed him to a screen door off the side of the house. "It will take all of two seconds to show you the pumpkin crop. It's just not that interesting to a nonfarmer, I'm afraid.''

Parker could spend a whole lot more time than that outside just staring at Noreen, never mind whatever she was coaxing from the earth. As she strode confidently across her land, he kept up, not seeing the Ferrari that had just parked next to her truck.

NOREEN AND HER stupid plants! Garrison fumed as he watched his stepsister lead Parker toward her precious pumpkin crop. She'd get the guy all involved in her planting schemes, and no doubt the developer would forget that he should be calculating the worth of the land. That was the reason Garrison had manipulated him into coming to their house, not to be charmed by Noreen.

He'd have to think of a way to broach his interest in selling his share of Cinderella Acres. Garrison's lips twisted. Without the six percent voting share the aunts' held, he was frustratingly unable to accomplish his goal. And they'd never vote their portion with him willingly.

Unless he had something they wanted…and they wanted nothing more than to stay in their cottages at Cinderella Acres forever. And a husband for Noreen, of course.

He squinted into the slowly descending sun, seeing Parker follow Noreen like a shadow. It was so irritating being forced to live on what Noreen chose to dole out to him, thanks to her father's will that had put her in charge of running the farm! Garrison's mother had only been able to squeeze forty-four percent of the holding for her son. And with the aunts always firmly aligned on Noreen's side, he was destined to live by their wishes. He was ruled by women.

Getting a job for himself never occurred to Garrison. He deserved better out of life than to have to work. All that stood between him and ready wealth was four women, a situation he would somehow overcome. Parker had to be good for something, he mused. The first order of the day would be to keep Parker's mind on business, not on Noreen.

He honked and waved in a friendly manner, completely satisfied with the guilty start in Noreen's posture even at this distance. She waved back reluctantly, but at least Parker wasn't staring down into her eyes like a lovesick student anymore. Garrison grinned and got out of his car. "It's okay," he whispered with a loving rub on the shiny red paint. "We've got ourselves a sucker, and it's just a matter of waiting for the right moment to mention selling my land. Then I can pay off those nasty creditors, and your loan, too," he told the Ferrari. The bill was due in a week or the bank would repossess the car. But Garrison wasn't worried about that. Noreen always worried about bills, but as a rule, he did not. She claimed that this year's crop of pumpkin was all the profit the farm would make; the corn and cotton crops would go to pay back the bank mortgage in two weeks' time. Why couldn't she see that they didn't need to live by the whims of nature, when they could live very well if they simply sold out?

He went inside to wash up for dinner and to give himself time to plot.

PARKER STARED DOWN at the winding vines with yellow trumpet-looking flowers, some starting to round into gourds. "So this is the bumper pumpkin crop."

"This is it." Noreen's voice was dry as she looked at her pride and joy. "This is the best it's been in five years."

She'd been right: it did take a farmer to appreciate what another farmer was pulling from the dry Texas ground. He cleared his throat. "Impressive."

"It is not," she said, laughing. "In September, this will all look so different you'd be astonished. I'll need a big truck to haul my pumpkins into market."

He stooped to examine the thready green trails. "Magic."

She knelt beside him to observe her handiwork. "What's magic?"

"What you do for a living. Enchanting living plants from seed, water and dirt. And somehow making a crop and a livelihood from it."

"Oh." She seemed embarrassed. "It's not magic. Just poor economics and refusing to let go of a dream."

He brushed the dirt off her hands slowly, one palm at a time. "I believe that letting go of dreams is worse economics."

"Really?" Her voice held hope as she looked over his cotton shirt and pressed khaki trousers. "You seem to be doing all right for yourself. Did you have a dream you held on to?"

"Well, I..." How could he say that the only dream he'd had lately was to see Meg grow up happy and secure? How did one achieve such results when two parents were touted to be so much better than one? And he was a single father, with little knowledge of what girls needed past the four-year-old stage. There'd be bras and he'd be lost; there'd be first kisses and he'd consider sending a squad car for her suitor; there'd be first love...and he wouldn't know how to tell her to get through it any better than he had. He hadn't. He'd fallen head over heels in love with Meg's mother. It had come as a shock that Lavinia preferred a long-haired, artsy type with no steady income to the love and lifestyle he'd given. Yet, Lavinia had pursued her dream, and maybe he couldn't fault her for that. He was over the first sting of her loving someone more than him. But how could she ever have left behind her own flesh and blood, her beautiful, tiny daughter who wrung his heart every day with her innocent love for her daddy?

"What's wrong?" Noreen asked.

He looked away from her searching eyes. "I was thinking how to answer your question. I really can't. Is that smoke?" he asked suddenly, squinting toward the white-brick farmhouse.

"Smoke?" Noreen whipped her head around. Brownish-gray smoke streamed out of a kitchen window. "Oh, my gosh! I should never have let Aunt Hattie cook dinner!" She took off, running like a gazelle. Parker followed, passing her to jerk the side door open and run in to get Meg out, who was still asleep on the diminutive navy sofa. He laid her on top of a patch of soft grass outside before dashing in to shoo out aunts.

There was flour everywhere, the dust of it rising from every surface. Three little old ladies stared at him as he stood coughing in the doorway, flour lining the wrinkles of their adorable faces and coating their glasses.

He took a gulp of air to stop the coughing. "Is everybody all right? What happened?"

"Just a small grease fire," Hattie answered. "I don't know how it happened. One minute I was cooking the chicken, and the next it was on fire! I put it out, though, with good old all-purpose flour."

She was so proud of her efforts that Parker forced himself not to smile. Noreen, however, wasn't inclined to let the matter go.

"You could have been hurt! Or burned the house down!"

"But we didn't," Hattie said in a quavering voice. "Everything came out just fine."

"Except for the chicken," Priscilla inserted in her practical-as-always tone.

"Dinner does appear to be a bit on the done side," Charlene offered in her optimistic assessment of life. "But maybe if we scrape off the burned parts…"

"It wouldn't leave much to eat if we did." Priscilla shook her head. "That chicken will just have to accept the trash can as its fate."

They all looked rather woebegonely at Noreen. Parker sensed that they'd been trying hard to be perfect hostesses to him, in order to further their plans where he and Noreen were concerned. "Meg and I will go into town and pick up fried chicken," he announced. "If that's all right with you, Noreen."

"You don't have to do that," she replied briskly. "We invited you, we will keep our end of the invitation."

"Nonsense. If you hadn't been kind enough to ask us home to dinner, I'd have asked you out, anyway. So the least I can do is spring for a bucket of chicken."

Noreen halted at his words. The aunts paused to stare at him. Parker searched through what he'd said carefully. Hattie appeared delighted, her fingers clapped to her doughy button mouth. Ah. He felt his neck flush through the open area of his cotton shirt as he realized he'd admitted he wanted to go out with Noreen. So much for the cover of looking at land for commercial real estate. He merely shrugged at her curious glance. "Yes or no?" he murmured.

"Yes, thank you. We'd love some Dumpy's Fried Chicken, preferably not blackened."

"Dumpy's?" Parker raised his brows.

"Yes. What we lovingly refer to as DFC around here. There's actually a chain of them starting up," she assured him when he didn't lower his brows. "They've got the other ones beat for fried chicken. Now," Noreen became all business, "I'll get these three washed up while you're gone." She reached for Hattie, but her grandmother swiftly pulled back, gently slapping at Noreen's hands.

"I can clean up my own mess, Noreen Cartwright.

You should accompany your gentleman caller to Dumpy's.''

"He's *not* my gentleman caller," Noreen said in a swift undertone, her eyes darting quickly to see if Parker had heard. He had, so he shrugged.

"You still should go with your guest," Hattie insisted.

"For once, I agree with Hattie," Priscilla said with a sigh.

"The drive into town is so pretty in the twilight," Charlene added, her tone waxing romantic. "And Parker can retrieve his car before our well-meaning sheriff tickets it."

"Oh, darn. Come on, Parker," Noreen said, a trifle ungraciously. "Where's Meg?"

"Oh, my gosh!" He strode out of the kitchen, worried that Meg might have awakened and wandered off during the excitement. His only thought had been to get her outside in case the house was on fire. To his relief, she still lay on the bed of soft grass where he'd placed her. A few purple clover flowers waved near her long hair, and Parker's chest filled with love for his beautiful daughter. How could his wife have ever left this treasure behind?

"She's so pretty," Noreen said from behind him.

"Like an angel," Hattie agreed, the only of Noreen's relatives to have followed them all the way outside. Charlene and Priscilla peered out the screen door, nodding. "Bring her back inside where she was, Parker. We can watch her while you go to the DFC— if you think you can trust us with your beautiful daughter."

"If you'll trust me with yours."

No matter that Noreen was actually a niece. Hattie

beamed at his compliment to Noreen and nodded happily.

"Yes, we most certainly will. Bring the child back inside. We'll take extra-good care of her, while you hunt up some edible dinner."

"It's a deal," he replied, well aware that Hattie was scheming again, but not bothered by it at all. There were good schemes in life and bad ones, and a good-hearted one was actually kind of fun. It was still just a magical Sunday afternoon, with no strings attached for him.

But it had a family sort of feeling about the whole thing, which was something he and Meg hadn't known in a very long time.

GARRISON LAZED on the sofa in front of the TV, listening to the loony relations excitedly discussing how wonderful Parker Walden was. Ah, Mr. Wonderful. Mr. Could-Do-No-Wrong. It was annoying! He pushed his tortoiseshell glasses up on his nose and continued plotting. Somehow he ought to be able to convince Noreen to sell Mr. Fabuloso the land. The trouble was those aunts, who were up to their pruny faces in plans for their precious Noreen. She was never going to sell the farm, no matter how poorly it was doing, as long as her family was taking up residence on the back forty. Three tiny houses for three tiny women. What a waste! But that was Noreen. Not one house, where all three of them could live together. Oh, no. They each had to have special architect plans, suiting each of their own various needs and personalities. That had been ten years ago, and Garrison still wanted to scream remembering the continuous ring of hammers and buzz of saws. He had nada, while everyone around him had everything they wanted.

He wanted the farm sold, and his money in his pocket. If that meant selling the tract of Cinderella Acres where the aunts lived, then so be it. For the millionth time, he wished his mother had been able to browbeat old man Cartwright out of more than she had. The old man had tied a provision into his will: not a square inch could be sold without Noreen and Garrison being in perfect agreement.

They would never, ever be in perfect agreement about anything.

"Whatcha doing?"

A childish voice startled him out of his dissatisfying musing and shot him to a sitting position. The hazel eyes of an inquisitive tot regarded him with interest. "What do you mean, what am I doing?" he demanded crustily. "Go into the kitchen and bother the old ladies."

"I want to watch TV with you." Meg got up beside him and peered at the game show he hadn't really been watching. "Where's Barney?"

"Barney?" Garrison put some distance between himself and the child by leaning away from her. "Who's that?"

"Barney the dinosaur. I want to see him."

Her voice had gotten a bit louder and more insistent. Garrison found himself immobilized by the unexpected turn of events. "I bet if you go into the kitchen, someone would give you a cookie," he bribed.

She considered for a moment. "I'll just stay with you and wait for Barney to come on."

"What channel is Barney's?" Garrison asked, his voice taut with the effort to be nice.

"PBS," she said with assurance. "If you give me the clicker, I can find it myself."

He handed the device to her, astounded by her dexterity with the "clicker." Unfortunately, only game and news shows were on.

"I can't find it," she said, greatly disappointed.

"Too bad," he said, not meaning it a bit.

"Miss Noreen said you'd give me a pony ride. Let's go do that instead!" she said, sitting up and clapping her slight hands with joy.

Oh, brother, Garrison groaned. He wanted nothing less on earth than to have to spend time with this child, actually any child. He could think of nothing more distasteful, and he cursed Noreen for actually mentioning his name in combination with a pony-riding excursion. "Listen, I'll pay you five dollars if you just go away," he promised her. "I don't want to take you pony riding, and—"

"Garrison!" Hattie looked down at him from behind the sofa with reproving, stern eyes rimmed by white flour. Puffs of dust frosted through her gray hair, giving her a rather comical appearance, but there was nothing humorous in the bantam stance of her posture. Hands on her hips, she demanded, "How dare you try to bribe a child?"

"I—I," he stuttered.

Meg's eyes were on him with soulful patience. "You're in trouble now," she informed him with childlike sincerity.

"I suggest you get the small saddle out," Hattie told him with authority. "And may I also suggest you remember that Meg is a guest in our home and should be treated as such?''

Garrison slowly stood, his entire body tense with anger. "Oh, come on," he said ungraciously to the disgusting brat.

"Meanie, Meanie, Meanie!" the child sang, jumping to her feet.

"I am not!" Garrison cried, stung. "I just don't like little—uh—" He stopped at the glare in Hattie's alert, dark eyes.

"I'm going to ride on Meanie!" Meg finished her impromptu song.

"Meanie is very gentle. You'll enjoy getting to know her." She directed a meaningful stare at Garrison. "Make certain you take very good care of Meg."

"Oh, fine!" He stalked out of the house with Meg running behind him, very aware that he'd just been reprimanded. The annoying battleaxes were always bossing him around. "Be nice to the guest in our home," he mimicked. Well, it wasn't their house. They might live at Cinderella Acres, but one day, he'd have them packing their bags.

Being nice to the land developer's brat was probably the best way to begin working on his goal.

"Meanie, Meanie, Meanie!" Meg shouted, running to the stalls.

Garrison began whistling to himself. Ponies and little girls went together like flowers and sunshine. And the way to Parker Walden's good side was, quite obviously, his child.

Chapter Four

"We're out of chicken," the teen at the counter in the local DFC informed Parker and Noreen twenty minutes later. The drive had been lovely in the country air, soothing Noreen. Hattie was so obvious in her intentions! Yet Parker appeared completely unfazed by the whole matter, and she'd been able to relax on the drive into town.

Until now. "What do you mean?" she demanded. "How can you be out of chicken?"

Parker was trying not to smile. Noreen saw nothing funny about the whole matter. It was one more incident to chalk up to the series of awkward ones since she'd met him.

The teen shrugged. "Truck didn't come in. Held up in traffic outside of Dallas."

"You have deep freezes and stock on hand, surely." Noreen was incredulous.

"Yep. But we went through it during Sunday lunch. Church crowd, ya know."

"I see." She sneaked a peek at Parker, who appeared to be trying not to laugh. "May I ask what is so funny?"

"Thanks, anyway," he said to the teen, steering

Noreen outside the small eatery. "It just is funny. I don't think we're meant to eat chicken today, do you?"

She thought about that, mainly noticing how his eyes twinkled when he smiled. "I suppose not. We're certainly not having much luck with it."

"Maybe we should just change our plans. Let's order some pizza instead. Will the aunts eat pizza?"

"Yes, but Garrison won't."

"We'll let him hunt up his own dinner." Parker helped Noreen into the driver's side of the truck and went around to let himself in the other side.

"Oh, I...couldn't do that to him." Noreen hesitated. "It might hurt his feelings."

"Okay."

Other than a glance her way, Parker didn't seem to question her worries. Noreen knew it sounded silly because Garrison was, after all, a grown man who could raid a fridge on his own. And he hadn't originally been in on the pseudo date the aunts had thoughtfully wrangled for Noreen. But she just couldn't leave Garrison out. "There's a diner in town that serves home-style food. What if we try there for some chicken? It's close to your car, too."

"Hey, three times is supposed to be the charm." Parker gave her an agreeable smile that made Noreen's heart thump in her chest. "Drive on."

"I appreciate you being so understanding about Garrison." She put the truck in gear and headed out onto the road into town. "I know people think I let him run over me, but he is my younger brother. He didn't get the chance to know my father for as long, and he lost his mother, too. I can't help worrying about him."

"There's nothing to be understanding about." Parker shrugged. "You've got a good heart, Noreen."

"Thank you." She smiled at him, wondering if there was a woman in his life who had a good heart, too. Though Parker wasn't wearing a ring, that didn't mean he wasn't wearing his heart on his sleeve for a lady in Dallas. It was none of her business, she thought with a pang. And it wouldn't matter if he weren't. They were from two different worlds, as evidenced by the nice clothes he wore, and the expensive Mercedes he'd pointed out in the parking lot in the town square as his. What could she offer him, anyway? She had a dusty, in-the-red farm and three sweet relatives bent on matchmaking.

All of that was guaranteed to run a man right off.

She wondered why Parker had hung around this long. Once again, she reminded herself not to be taken in by a charmingly packaged male. For all she knew, the man had reasons of his own for dallying in Rockwall—reasons which could very well have more to do with Garrison's hint about real estate than being nice to three elderly ladies and their farmer goddaughter.

"I TOLD YOU your meddling was going to backfire, Hattie Mayes," Priscilla said darkly. "Just look at the mess you've made."

"Oh, fiddle." Hattie stared into the burner, noticing that the silver foil underneath the stove eye would have to be changed. "It got away from me before I could stop it," she explained, meaning the unfortunate flames that had burst up over the sides of the skillet before she'd had time to blink.

"I'd say Noreen could do with a little less of your

fairy godmother interference and a little more mind-your-own-business." Priscilla got a broom to sweep the flour that decorated the yellowed linoleum.

"Hattie didn't mean to start a grease fire." Charlene rushed to her sister's defense. "Goodness, it could happen to anyone, Priscilla."

"Yes, but mostly to a busybody who's got things on her mind other than the chicken she's supposed to be frying. If good cooking was the way you meant to catch that city boy, Hattie, you blew it."

"Oh, dear." Hattie straightened, her mouth pulled down sadly. "I can't help but agree with you, Priscilla. I *am* disaster-prone. My good aim appears to have gone awry." She felt like sitting down and having a good cry about the matter. What else was a good godmother-aunt supposed to do in life, if not help her lovely goddaughter win a prince of a man? Sniffling to herself, Hattie decided maybe she'd lost her touch after all. "I do *so* want to be a help."

"Well, it turned out just fine, if you ask me," Charlene said.

"All right, Miss Optimistic, just how do you figure that?" Priscilla stopped sweeping long enough to stare at both of her sisters.

"Well, the purpose of us cooking was to get Noreen alone with Parker. They are alone now, even as they fetch the meal." Charlene waited hopefully for their response. "Don't you agree? Meg is keeping Garrison out of trouble, we're in here doing good deeds, and our young lady is out with a fellow whom we suspect is a good egg. He didn't even have to ask her out, and Noreen didn't have to be goaded into accepting a date. It's all turned out for the best," she reiterated. "Of course, what would be better is another chance coincidence that just happened to keep them together a little longer—without them realizing it, you know. Still, we have to be grateful for grease fires,'' she said, wandering absently from the kitchen. ''I'm going to wash up.''

Hattie sat straight in the chair, her mind going a mile a minute.

''Oh, no, you don't,'' Priscilla warned. ''I know that gleam in your eyes. You pay no attention whatsoever to the feathers in Charlene's head. She always has something positive to say, even when she's flat wrong. She was just trying to make you feel better for the disaster you single-handedly contrived.''

''I know,'' Hattie agreed, but not really listening at all to her elder sibling. Priscilla had such a tendency to be peremptory, though she meant well. Charlene was right to try to turn bad things into good, and maybe that was the surest mark of a wonderfully talented godmother, Hattie decided. Her gaze suddenly narrowed in determination on the white porcelain, flower-painted teapot on the stove. ''But you know, Priscilla, we really should always be grateful for small disasters.''

NOREEN LET PARKER drive her truck on the way over to his car so that she could hold the bags of chicken, mashed potatoes, gravy and assorted side dishes they'd ordered. She'd insisted he drive and she balance the sacks, mainly because, she said, she was afraid the gravy might leak and soil his khakis. He'd told her a little gravy wouldn't ruin his evening, but she'd smiled and handed him her keys.

To be honest, driving her made him feel as if they actually were on a date. It was a strange sensation he found himself enjoying, to the point that he nearly reached over and caught her fingers in his. He reminded himself her hands were full enough, and that touching her would probably be bad for both of them. No sense taking matters places they weren't destined to go.

It was one enchanted night only. After the dinner bell had rung and been retired for the evening, he and Meg would go back to Dallas the same as they'd been before their visit to Rockwall: a fairly lonely father and daughter making it the best they could, each trying to figure out why the woman they both had loved had left them behind.

"THIS SMELLS WONDERFUL." Fifteen minutes later, Parker and Noreen were back at Cinderella Acres. They'd gotten out of their respective vehicles and now stood beside the split-rail fence watching Meg enjoy her pony ride. Noreen looked down into one of the bags. "You'll love the gravy Mrs. Morrison fixes to go with the potatoes."

"I believe it."

She glanced up at him. "Are you always this nice? This agreeable?"

He shook his head at the inquiring expression in her eyes. "No way. Ask my daughter how nice I am when she wants something and I tell her no."

"Are you a strict parent?" Her voice held laughter, as if his being strict was impossible.

"Not strict. Just firm." He was silent for a moment before sighing. "About the time my daughter reached two and a half, her...my, um, wife left. We began suffering increased doses of the terrible twos."

"Really?" Noreen's eyes and tone turned sympathetic. "Poor Meg."

"Well, that's what I thought, too, for the first couple of months. Here was my poor daughter with no mother for guidance. I'm afraid I let her push all my buttons for guilt." He smiled ruefully, remembering. "Every toy she saw, any piece of candy she demanded in the grocery aisle, I bought to make up for my marriage falling apart and robbing her of her mother. All it got me was one very spoiled little lady."

"What did you do?"

"We sat down and had a long talk about how much we missed Mommy, but that Mommy wasn't going to come back. Since it was just the two of us, we'd have to get along together. And that from then on, if she pitched fits, she'd have to be punished."

"Did it work?" Noreen was breathless from wanting to hear more of Parker's story. For one thing she had learned that he was essentially a free man. But for another it was simply wonderful hearing honest emotion from a man. Garrison had never been one for much directness, and Noreen loved hearing Parker talk about his real feelings.

"Look at her." He gestured with his head toward a paddock where a disgruntled-looking Garrison led a pony to an imperious Meg's instructions. Her piping voice carried clearly to the open truck window, as she urged the pony to go, "Faster! Faster!"

"Does she appear to be a child who doesn't expect to get her way about most everything?"

Noreen laughed. "I think you've done a wonderful job with her," she told him, making his chest feel about two sizes larger. "She's darling. And considering the circumstances, it probably won't hurt her to be a bit spoiled anyway.''

"I hope not. I haven't finished completely reining her in." He turned from watching Meg to stare into Noreen's wonderfully deep and understanding blue-denim eyes. "My ex pops in and out of our lives infrequently so Meg is used to it, but I'm afraid the situation concerns me for her sake."

It wasn't that he missed his wife anymore; he missed the family he'd thought they were going to have. What did he tell a four-year-old about the whims of women who decided they weren't cut out to be mothers?

"Well, she'll certainly be tuckered out after her excursion today." Noreen's smile was soft and warm for him. "Let's get you some dinner. I bet Meg is hungry, and before you know it, it'll be her bedtime."

He could barely think about it. He didn't want to leave. But he took the largest of the sacks from Noreen and carried it inside the house that had inexplicably begun to feel like a haven to him—and Meg.

MOMENTS LATER all seven of them were seated around the oak kitchen table. Meg sat between Parker and Noreen, an arrangement that suited Noreen fine. The child with the long, dark curly hair and big eyes had certainly touched her heart in a way she had never expected. Never mind that she'd never dreamed her heart would be so affected by Meg's big, strong daddy....

"More potatoes, Noreen?" Hattie asked. "Put some on Meg's plate. She's eating so well!" Hattie beamed at the child, and Meg beamed back.

Garrison sighed loudly and unexpectedly.

"Something wrong with your food, Garrison?" Priscilla inquired.

"No."

His curt reply was at odds with his handsome appearance. Noreen had always thought her stepbrother resembled a famous movie star. *If only appearances weren't so deceiving,* she thought sadly. But Garrison was her burden to bear, something she'd accepted when her father had died.

"Did you think you'll be buying any land around here, Parker?" Garrison suddenly asked eagerly.

The entire table of diners went still and quiet. Noreen's shoulders tensed painfully.

"I haven't given it much thought, actually." Parker smiled at Garrison in a friendly fashion, but didn't appear to be interested in discussing business. Noreen's shoulders relaxed.

"The land behind ours is for sale. I hope Noreen pointed that out to you," Garrison mentioned, his eyes penetrating.

"Actually, she did." Beneath the table, Parker squeezed Noreen's hand, an action which surprised and pleased her. For the first time she realized he was on her side—or at least trying to be. Meg's foot kicked jerkily as she shifted in her chair, and Noreen felt Parker's hand move to pat his daughter's leg.

Noreen felt her heart turn inward with poignant longing. She forced her attention back to her plate, but her appetite was gone.

She really, really liked this man. His kindness and honesty was wooing a heart she had long ago decided not to give any man.

"Part of the Cartwright holding is mine," Garrison blurted on a rush. "You wouldn't happen to know anyone who'd be interested in developing a parcel of land like this one, would you?''

Hattie's, Charlene's and Priscilla's forks clattered against the every-day china. Noreen gripped hers so hard she felt the stainless steel marking her fingers. How dare her stepbrother even think such a thing? Angry dismay rose inside her.

"I'm afraid not." Parker managed to look apologetic yet interested at the same time. "You see, this land is earmarked for residential development only. I deal in commercial real estate."

"I...see." It was clear by his disappointment that he did not. "What does that mean, exactly?"

"It means that you can sell to another person who wants to live here, but not to someone who wants to build, say, a grocery store on it."

"You mean I'm stuck?" Garrison gave up all pretense of interest in the fried chicken on his plate. "Nobody else would want it?"

"Well, they might want the land for farming." Parker appeared to consider the situation. "But it's out of my area of expertise, Garrison. I'm sorry."

No one moved for a few moments. "Excuse me. I think I'll go outside," Garrison said, abruptly leaving the table.

Noreen frowned slightly at Parker. Nothing about what he'd just said to Garrison rang true to her. But his demeanor was blithe as he fed Meg a spoonful of peas, and Noreen told herself to relax. She didn't feel like eating anymore, though.

Either Parker had lied to Garrison for a reason—or he wasn't the real estate developer he'd pretended to be.

"WE HAD A GREAT TIME," Parker said to the four women. He had a tired Meg in his arms, and the hour was late. As much as he hated to leave, the wonderful day was over. "Thank you for your hospitality."

"Nonsense." Hattie was brisk. "Thank you for providing dinner, and for sharing Meg with us." She patted Meg's hand. "'Bye, sweetie."

Priscilla and Charlene said goodbye, as well. That left Parker standing alone with Noreen. "Thank you for having us out."

Lamplight fell softly on her pretty face as her lips turned up in a small smile. "You're welcome. But, Parker, before you go, there's something I have to know. Why did you tell Garrison that about our farm?"

He shrugged, and Meg leaned into his shoulder the way Noreen would love to. It looked so comforting, so protective...

"Because I figured he didn't know any better. I thought he might just be fishing to get your goat. Besides, I don't get into private family situations. And don't quote me on any of the facts I was spouting. I'd just always heard it wasn't good to mix business with pleasure, and I considered eating dinner with your family to be pleasure. I was kind of making up my story as I went along."

Noreen's heart bloomed back to the generous, happy size it had been a couple hours before Garrison's surprise inquiry had thrown a wrench into her emotions. "Thank you."

"You're welcome."

He stepped off the porch, and Noreen ignored the puzzling thought that the moment didn't feel right without him kissing her good-night. He didn't say he'd call her, but that would have sounded awkward to both of them. Yet, her heart desperately wanted to know if she'd ever see him and his sweet little girl again.

He turned back. "I didn't fool *you*, though, did I?"

She shook her head. "No. You didn't. You did have me worried about what kind of developer you were."

He grinned at her. Going to his car, he tucked Meg securely into her booster seat and buckled her in. He got into the driver side with one more reluctant wave to Noreen.

Almost as if he's going to miss me. But that couldn't be possible. They didn't know each other well enough. Yet, the strange, heavy feeling in her heart told her that time and feelings weren't weighing in equal measure.

He started the car, which died with an ominous whirr. Her jaw dropped as she listened to him try the ignition again.

This time there was no sound at all.

Chapter Five

"Is something wrong?" Noreen called from the porch. The Mercedes looked almost new. It was supposed to be a reputable brand, so she couldn't imagine why it wouldn't start.

"I'm not sure," Parker called out the window. "I'll try again." He turned the key, but the car didn't so much as sputter.

"Shall I get a flashlight?" Noreen asked.

"If you don't mind." He got out of the car and raised the hood.

"Is he having a problem with his car?" Hattie came to the door with a flashlight. "We heard you mention that you needed this."

Of course. The kitchen windows were open as always, and Noreen was glad Parker hadn't kissed her good-night after all.

Glad—but wistful, too.

"Thank you, Aunt Hattie." Noreen took the flashlight. "I'm certain it's something easily fixed."

Five minutes later Parker flexed his shoulders in resignation. "I can't see what would keep it from starting. All the cables are connected, nothing appears to be missing." He sighed heavily, embarrassed. "If I can borrow a phone, I'll call a tow truck."

The three elderly women hovered around his car, peering under the hood with interest.

"It won't do you any good to call a wrecker at this time of night," Hattie informed him. "None of the garages are open."

"Oh." He wouldn't have thought twice about calling for help in Dallas. "Do you have any suggestions?"

They were all quiet for a moment.

"You can spend the night here," Hattie said. "It's the obvious thing to do."

Parker shook his head. "You've been too kind already. There has to be a motel in town where we can stay."

"Your little girl would be better off here," Priscilla observed.

"We must consider Noreen's reputation," Charlene mentioned. "Will it look bad if her gentleman caller spends the night with her?"

Discomfort made Parker's neck hot. He couldn't bear to look at Noreen to see how she was taking the conversation. The aunts were doing their darnedest to get them together, and if he didn't know better, he would suspect they'd sabotaged his car.

"My reputation will be just fine." Noreen's voice rang with authority in the night. "Garrison is here, after all. And if people care more about my personal life than helping someone with car trouble, so be it. Parker, unstrap Meg and carry her inside. She's two seconds away from falling asleep."

He hesitated, staring into her eyes for any sign of

reluctance. "Are you sure? I don't want to cause you any more problems than I already have."

"You haven't caused me any problem at all," she said softly.

He sighed, still uncertain.

"Daddy! Let me out!" Meg called.

"Okay, sweetie. Hang on." He went around and unstrapped his daughter. "I just can't imagine what went wrong with my car. It was fine not two hours ago."

"Well, we'll take a better look at it in the morning." Noreen held the front door open for him so he could carry Meg through. "Take her upstairs, and you can share the yellow bedroom on the right."

"Oh, hurray!" Meg squirmed out of her father's arms and ran up the wide staircase. She ran back down the stairs and then went back up.

"Stairs. A novelty." Parker smiled weakly at Noreen, his ego still smarting from his car breaking down.

"Of course. They were for me when I was small, too."

"I want to sleep in this room! Come see, Daddy!"

"Now wait, honey," he said, following her upstairs. "This isn't a hotel."

He stopped where his daughter stood transfixed. The bed Meg was gazing at was completely white, with lace everywhere. Lace hung from the top of a large four-poster bed; it covered the pillows in demure flower patterns and hung from the mattress edge in delicate swaths. Red and pink tulips were scattered across the walls, giving the room a wonderfully old-fashioned feeling.

"It's pretty, isn't it?" he said to Meg.

"Thank you." Noreen smiled at both of them. "Hattie, Charlene and Priscilla took great care in surprising me with this. Decorating isn't something I have a lot of time, or interest in, I'm afraid."

Parker's throat went instantly dry. Noreen's bedroom! This tall, competent, gorgeous woman went to bed every night in a room designed for a princess.

How he would love to raid her ivory tower!

"Come on, sweetie. Let's see what our room looks like."

Meg stared at him with big, entreating eyes. "I want to sleep with Miss Noreen, Daddy."

He did, too, but that was out of the question—for both of them. "Honey, you and I will sleep together tonight. Kind of a special occasion. Okay?" Turning, he waited for Noreen to point him to the bedroom.

Smiling, she showed them to the one she'd called the yellow room. It had daffodil sprays trailing across the wallpaper. The bedspread continued the effect with yellow flowers and green stems.

"I still want to sleep with Miss Noreen," Meg insisted.

"Let me get you a T-shirt to sleep in, Meg," Noreen said, "although I'm afraid it's going to be big. And Garrison's got something you can sleep in, I'm sure, Parker."

She glanced over his frame doubtfully and Parker winced. He was about four inches taller than her stepbrother and a lot more muscular. Besides, he didn't want to borrow anything from a man who didn't appear to have his sister's—or aunts'—best interests at heart. "That's all right," he said swiftly. "I'm just as happy sleeping in T-shirt and boxers."

"Are you certain?" She reached down to run one

hand gently through Meg's long hair. "There's no point in being uncomfortable."

He was uncomfortable with the fact that his car had betrayed him, but he'd be more than that if she went and got something of Garrison's for him. "I'm fine, really. Thanks."

"We're going now, Noreen, dear," Hattie called up the stairs. "Good night, Meg. Good night, Parker."

He went to the landing. "Good night, all. Sorry about this latest development."

"Think nothing of it," Hattie said airily. "We'll walk over in the morning and make you some pancakes. Don't believe even I can mess up pancakes." She waved, and the three sisters departed.

"Well," he said to Noreen, "good night, I guess."

"Good night." Her voice was soft. "Be sure to put Meg in the T-shirt I laid on the bed, and there are guest toothbrushes in the bathroom in your room."

"Gotcha."

"Good night," she repeated.

They stood staring at each other for a moment. Meg stood beside her daddy's leg, almost on his foot, her gaze curious.

"Are you going to kiss her good-night?" she asked.

Both adults laughed a little self-consciously. Noreen backed into the hall, the spell broken. "See you in the morning."

"'Night." He smiled and closed the door after her.

"You didn't kiss her." Meg sounded disappointed.

"I really didn't think I should." He drew her dress over her head so he could put the T-shirt on her. The shirt was small, but not small enough, so he put a knot in each shoulder to keep her feet from tangling in it in the night. The stray thought that Noreen had worn it put a lump in his throat.

"Don't you think she's pwetty?"

"I do. But I can't kiss every pretty girl I meet, can I?" He kissed her on each cheek and scooted her up into bed.

"No. But I think it would be all right to kiss *her*," Meg opined. "She'd be a good mommy for us."

"A good...mommy?" Parker was momentarily perplexed, before he realized that Meg had confused mother and wife as something they were both missing. She meant a good wife for him, and a good mommy for her—in other words, a good replacement for the thing they lacked in their lives.

He couldn't help wondering if she was right. The trouble was, substituting one wrong woman for another would be devastating to Meg, and to him.

It was a risk he wasn't willing to take—for either of their sakes.

As was their custom, Hattie, Priscilla and Charlene navigated their way on foot across the flat field that separated their houses from Noreen's. "You couldn't have planned that any better if you'd tried, Hattie," Priscilla said, "though I hope we won't regret this in the morning."

"Why would we?" Hattie didn't care much for her sister's tone.

"There could be consequences to nights spent alone together between two people who don't know each other well." Priscilla filled her words with ominous dread.

"Oh, for heaven's sake." Hattie felt very cross,

and the fact that Charlene hadn't jumped in with her usual words of positive thinking to counteract Priscilla's always-negative ones vexed her. "You act like they're really going to sleep with each other."

"They are. In the same house. In my day—" Priscilla began.

"In our day we weren't struggling to keep a farm together with our own two hands, as well as take care of three elderly relatives and a lazy stepbrother. Noreen doesn't have time to meet eligible bachelors," Hattie interrupted. "Besides, they're not going to sleep together in the Biblical sense, so there's nothing for you to get your nose out of joint over. And Noreen is a grown woman, quite capable of saying no if pressed, though I doubt the question will arise." She hmmphed to herself, quite put out with Priscilla's naysaying. "Oh, my heavens!" she exclaimed.

"What is it now?" Priscilla and Charlene chorused.

"Nothing." Hattie couldn't believe she'd nearly forgotten. "You two go on ahead without me. I'll follow in a moment."

"No more meddling," Priscilla instructed, "and we'll wait for you at your house. If we don't see you in fifteen minutes, I'm calling Noreen to hunt you up."

"Fine, fine." Hattie waved absently and headed back toward the farmhouse. She went into the kitchen and quietly took the white, flower-patterned tea kettle from the stove, where she filled it at the sink with lukewarm water. Silently, she crept out front and gingerly lifted the hood on Parker's Mercedes. For just a second, she illuminated the battery with the flashlight she'd nabbed, and carefully poured water from the tea kettle into it. "All full again," she murmured. Inch by inch, she lowered the hood, dusting off her hands afterward. "There," she said with great satisfaction, "one more small disaster for which we can be thankful."

NOREEN HAD TROUBLE falling asleep, though she rarely suffered sleeplessness once she was in her cozy bed. Thinking about Parker kept her wide awake. Could he be the man she'd waited for all her life?

And she *had* been waiting. In college, she had known her future, and it didn't include the typical rat race for a husband that some of her sorority sisters engaged in. She had always known the farm would be her only mate, particularly after lung disease had robber her father's skin of the tan he'd always had from working outdoors. Studying all the harder, she'd graduated in three years—with honors—in order to come home and help hold down the fort.

The ranch was still her only mate. She didn't think many men could understand her work, which brought her home dirty and dusty after twelve-hour workdays. There wasn't any time left over for her to make a home and devote the time to a spouse, maybe even children. For example, Meg. It was dangerous territory, but she allowed her mind to dreamily cross into it. If she was Meg's stepmother, there'd be homeroom mothering, Brownies, school field trips—all the things she would want to do for a child of hers.

As a matter of fact, she'd love doing all that. But as long as she had the farm, she couldn't plan on being home much. She didn't even have a cell phone so that she could be reached easily. It was long days—longer during harvest season—just her and the crops and the constant worry about the bank balance. And three little ladies who depended upon her. Garrison, too, represented a drag on her for his allowance. Not that she wasn't grateful for her farm, but it didn't leave a whole lot left over for nurturing a family.

A sudden soft and low sound pulled Noreen from her bed. Hesitating outside the yellow guest room door, she listened to Meg crying and Parker's deep voice comforting his daughter.

Gently, Noreen knocked on the door before opening it part way. "Are you two all right in here?"

The sight of Parker's tousled hair and bare chest as he held his daughter in his arms made Noreen swallow through a suddenly tight throat. He'd said he was going to sleep with his T-shirt on!

"We've just had a little nightmare," he told her. His gaze roved appreciatively from her ankles back to her face, and instantly, Noreen realized she hadn't grabbed her housecoat. She wore an ankle-length, rose cotton T-shirt that was baggy enough, and comfortable, but that seemed to have Parker's attention.

She decided she liked having his attention.

"Can I do anything to help you?" she asked.

"No." He shook his head. "We have these periodically."

Meg looked up at Noreen through teary eyes, and she felt her heart contract. These two people were in a situation she couldn't even imagine. She had her aunts and Garrison, who, even if he wasn't much of a brother, she still held out hope for.

Parker and Meg had no one except each other. She had the feeling they were adrift, clinging to the remnants of their family life. It broke her heart! As much as she'd love to be the solution for them, Noreen knew beyond a shadow of a doubt that she had little to offer.

She sighed heavily. "You know, Meg, when I was a little girl and I couldn't sleep, I used to go get up in my dad's bed. We'd watch late-night movies, mostly old, scary black-and-white ones, which, looking back on it, probably weren't very appropriate for me. But I loved them." She and her father had watched every Frankenstein movie, every mummy flick ever made. That was before he'd married Garrison's mother, and another kind of not-so-fun horror had entered their home.

"Nowadays, though, there is the magic of cable." Noreen forced her voice to sound happy and her mind not to remember the unhappy times so that she could concentrate on her guests. She raised her eyebrows at Parker. "Would cartoons be soothing?"

He nodded, a hesitant smile lining his lips. Noreen turned to pull the small TV on a rolling cart nearer the bed and switched it on with the remote. The room lit with the soft, comforting glow of cartoon colors. "See?" she said quietly as the little mouse began besting the big cat on the screen. "There's nothing to cry about, Meg." She smiled at the little girl, who instantly pulled away from her daddy to tug the sheets down next to her.

"Sit here," she commanded.

"Oh, no. I couldn't," Noreen said with a nervous glance toward Parker.

"I want you to stay with me." Meg's eyes were large with the plea. "Please, Miss Noreen?"

"I—" Noreen looked at Parker.

"I don't mind company, if that's what's worrying you."

"Well, I—" She wasn't worried. She just didn't know that getting into bed with him was a good idea! Noreen eyed the edge of the bed. "Maybe for a minute, but *just* a minute," she warned Meg. "I have to be up early in the morning, long before you've even opened your eyes, to check on my fields."

"Okay." Meg's voice was sunny as if everything was right in her world again. Her eyes were focused on the TV. As Noreen scooted in next to her, Meg curled up on her shoulder. Noreen froze for a second. Parker was on the *other* side of Meg, after all. Nothing could be more innocent, she assured herself. She'd stay for thirty minutes and give this child the security she craved and then creep back to her own bed. Nobody moved or said anything, and after a while she felt herself melting into the sheets and her eyelids growing heavy.

"It's like being a family again, Daddy," Noreen heard as she felt herself drifting off to sleep.

Noreen wanted to protest. Her good sense told her to flee into her own room. But Meg was right. It *was* like being a family again—and she had missed it as much as Meg.

Chapter Six

"My stars!" Hattie stared into the guest room, astonished by what she saw. Charlene and Priscilla peered over her shoulder. The TV was running, a soft hum of Looney Toons, not disturbing the three snoozers in the big bed. Noreen, who hadn't been visible in the fields this morning—which was why Hattie had decided a well-meaning check in her room was in order—lay on her side, under the covers. Meg was in the middle, her forehead barely touching Noreen's and her hand flung over her daddy. Parker slept turned toward the middle, his arm protectively over both Noreen and Meg. One nicely muscled and slightly hairy leg poked out from under the covers. The seamed edge of yellow, happy-face-printed boxers, most likely a recent Father's Day gift from Meg, left no doubt that he was "decent."

"They slept together!" Priscilla whispered in dismay.

"But not in the Biblical sense!" Hattie swiftly reiterated. "For heaven's sake, anyone with one eye in their head can see the whole thing is perfectly innocent!" She backed her sisters away from the door, particularly Charlene, who was still staring, her mouth wide open as if she'd seen a ghost.

"Maybe we should wake Noreen up," Charlene fretted.

"Nonsense." With crisp motions, Hattie ushered her sisters downstairs. She had never seen Noreen look so peaceful, so content. Nobody was waking her while Hattie had breath left in her body—unless Parker cared to do it with a kiss.

"It'll be very awkward for Noreen to find herself in bed with a man first thing in the morning." Charlene's eyes were wide with apprehension.

"It'll make matters more awkward if Noreen knows we know that they occupied the same bed. There'll be explanations and excuses, and quite frankly, I'd like to live under the illusion that they wanted to sleep together." She blithely continued her search for the box of pancake mix.

"Hattie Mayes!" Priscilla cried. "What has gotten into you? Pastor Jenkins would be mortified to hear you encouraging wanton behavior!"

"Pastor Jenkins will be more mortified if he never gets to perform a wedding ceremony for Noreen. It's high time that girl got off the shelf, by means fair or foul. Charlene, quit worrying and start cooking. I can't do everything myself." Hattie set to measuring milk and water. She had done her best to get a good, solid, first meeting for her goddaughter and this very eligible bachelor.

The rest was up to Noreen.

GARRISON STUMBLED bleary-eyed out of his bedroom on the second level, grouchy at being roused from sleep by the hissing voices of the old ladies. They

were clustered around the yellow guest bedroom like
a gaggle of startled geese, their gray heads focused
on something inside the room so that they didn't see
him. Whatever it was sure had them in a flap, though.
When they hurried downstairs on stealthy feet, Garrison scratched his head and decided he'd better take
a look at what had them so enthralled.

His jaw dropped at the sight of his sister in bed
with a man. Never mind that there was a child firmly
sandwiched in between and obviously no hanky-
panky had been entertained. He didn't think Noreen
had ever had a man in the house, let alone brought
one in to sleep with! Scratching his beard-stubbled
chin, Garrison, too, crept away from the guest room
and went into his own room to think. What if this
wealthy dude decided to marry Noreen? She would
never sell the farm. But if they got together, that was
one more person who would have his hands in the
cookie jar. Texas was a community property state, but
Garrison's share was Garrison's share. Nobody could
take that away from him, he comforted himself, because old man Cartwright's will was the law by which
Garrison and Noreen lived. His problem was liqui-
dating his assets, which brought him back to Parker.

One more man under this roof meant Garrison definitely would be a third wheel. He'd almost have to
find another place to live. Noreen never insisted he
get a job, but he'd almost be too embarrassed not to
with Parker strutting around with his goody-two-
shoes, nauseating niceness.

He didn't like that idea at all. It was one thing for
the land developer not to have seen the prime opportunity Garrison was offering, but it was a whole different scenario for Noreen and Parker to become so

close that Garrison got moved out of his cushy situation. Not to mention that creepy child might one day be living in the house, no doubt always after him for pony rides. Ugh! There was only so much he was willing to do to keep himself in the aunts' good graces, and stepping around horse droppings to make a child happy wasn't one of them.

He'd give Parker one more chance to see what a gold mine he was being offered.

If he rejected him again, Garrison decided, he'd just have to throw a kink into the old ladies' obvious bid for a prince for their Cinderella.

"THE PANCAKES turned out nicely, if I do say so myself." Hattie beamed at the group seated around the table, obviously pleased that no disasters had erupted. Sunshine streamed in the window, brightening the kitchen with early-morning light. Everyone had a smile on their face—except Garrison, Noreen noticed, which was typical. But she wasn't going to allow him to spoil her day. She'd awakened to find Parker's arm resting on her, and for one second before she'd crawled out of bed, she'd allowed herself to enjoy the masculine comfort.

It was probably the closest she'd ever get to really knowing what the marriage bed was like.

Then she'd pressed a light kiss against Meg's forehead, enjoying the feeling of soft baby skin against her lips. It was so tempting to fantasize about loving this child as her own....

But it was just a fantasy, and Noreen had made herself slip out of the bed and go into her own room to dress.

She should have been out in the fields long before

now. But she couldn't resist a few more moments with Parker. Now breakfast was over, the dishes were being cleared away, and it was time to say goodbye. She bit her lip to keep the disappointment from spoiling her smile.

"The pancakes were delicious, ladies," Parker agreed. "But we've got to hit the road. I'm going to go try my car one last time before I call the roadside assistance number."

He left the table and Noreen followed him. Meg stayed at the table for another super-sticky helping of pancakes and some spoil time with Hattie, Charlene and Priscilla.

"I'm glad I got to talk to you alone." He came to a stop beside the car. "We don't have a whole lot of opportunities to talk privately."

"Not with this bunch." Noreen had to smile at the truth of it. "We're well chaperoned."

"And you fell asleep on me last night."

That brought a laugh from her. "I did not!"

"You did. Right at the end of the first cartoon, in fact. I'm not even sure you saw Jerry give Tom his just desserts."

"I apologize. It had been an exciting day." She smiled in spite of the apology. "We don't usually have so much going on around here."

"I don't know if I believe you, not with those women in there. They keep things pretty lively." He rubbed the back of his neck. "It's pretty last minute, I know, but since I only met you yesterday…that sounds weird, doesn't it?"

She nodded in wry agreement. "Yes. Somehow, I feel that we've known each other a lot longer."

"Well, long enough to ask you for a favor, then.

Uh, a date.'' He winced. ''I'm not doing this very well, but I'm rustier than I thought I was.''

''I'm rusty myself,'' she said softly.

He took a deep breath. ''Thanks. You make me feel better.''

They smiled at each other for a long moment.

''There's a charity function this weekend I have to attend. It's a fund-raiser held by a commercial real estate association I belong to. I had planned on going stag, but if you're not doing anything, I'd love to have your company.''

''Would I be safe?'' she teased.

''Safe?''

''Little ol' me in a roomful of developers and real estate agents?''

He laughed. ''We'll tell them you're a school-teacher, or a flight attendant. Maybe a model. Anything but a farmer.''

''But I'm proud of being a farmer!''

''You should be. We'll tell everyone you're my real live date and not a prospect. Not in the real estate sense, anyway.'' His gaze was reassuring. ''It'll be okay, Noreen. I won't let anything happen to you. Join me for a night of small talk and overrated food in the name of charity.''

She tried to smile. ''The party sounds so fancy.'' This worried her. She had never attended something that required more than a church dress.

''It's black tie. So it is formal, but don't feel like you have to overdo it. No matter what you wear,'' he said, his hazel eyes glowing as he smiled at her, ''you'll be beautiful to me.''

Noreen's heart nearly melted out of her rib cage. ''Can I get back to you about this?'' She had to check her closet! There were shoes, accessories and other things that would have to go along with such an occasion, and a spending spree wasn't in her budget.

"Sure." He shrugged easily. "I'll call you tonight."

"Okay." Noreen liked the sound of that.

He slid into the car, keeping the door open. "This car has never been unreliable. It's never even had a flat." He stuck the key in the ignition and turned it. The car sputtered, as if trying to remember what it was supposed to do. He tried again, and it roared to life. "Amazing! It wouldn't do a thing for me last night."

Noreen shook her head at him. "I remember. But I'm kind of glad it didn't." She blushed, afraid she sounded silly. "Let me get Meg for you. You keep it running. I'm afraid if you turn it off, it won't start again, and at least this way you'll be closer into town if it quits again."

"Thanks."

She flew off to get Meg, who was thoroughly doused in syrup. "Let me wash you off, sweetie. Your daddy's going to take you home."

"I don't want to go," the little girl said plaintively, her gaze adoring as she looked at Noreen. "Please let me stay."

"Oh, Meg." Noreen hesitated with the rinsing. "Your daddy would be so sad and lonely without you...and you can come another day. Okay?"

"Okay." Meg slid down from Noreen's arms and allowed Hattie to dry her off with a dish towel. Then Meg hugged Noreen's knees. "I had a good time."

"Oh!" Noreen glanced at Hattie, startled.

"Good manners," Hattie said approvingly. "She

comes from good stock.'' Priscilla and Charlene nodded their agreement, and Meg hugged each one of
them before she ran out to her daddy's car, her long,
wavy hair flying behind her.

Noreen followed, amazed to see Garrison standing
by the Mercedes. He and Parker appeared to be engaged in conversation, even as Parker strapped his
daughter into the car seat. Surely her stepbrother
wasn't trying to railroad Parker into a business discussion again!

As soon as he saw her, Garrison put an engaging
smile on his face. ''Think about it,'' he said, before
loping off.

''Think about what?'' Noreen asked, coming to
stand where her stepbrother had been.

''The same thing. Your stepbrother wants to sell
out his part of the farm. That doesn't come as a surprise to you, does it?''

Noreen allowed her gaze to travel over Parker's
dark, neatly cut hair and his strong forehead and chin.
This wasn't a man who allowed other people to sway
him, she told herself. ''No part of the farm is for
sale,'' she told him firmly. ''Not a foot.''

''You'd better tell *him*.'' Parker jerked his head in
the direction that Garrison had gone. ''He might find
a buyer the way he's going at it.''

''I think he's just hounding you because he knows
you're in real estate development.''

''Maybe. But you are sitting on a prime tract of
land, with easy access to the highway, Noreen. The
land in back of those three houses is zoned for commercial. The way this town is growing, I'd keep it in
mind. Your zoning could easily be changed to com-

mercial, and if he wants a buyer, he'll find one easily enough.''

"We don't need a buyer," she said stiffly.

"Can he get around you?"

"No." Her tone brooked no further inquiry.

He sighed heavily. "Sorry. It's none of my business. But if he approached me, he'll approach someone else. I just thought you should know."

Meg sat still, frozen by the fractious tone in the adults' voices. Noreen didn't want to upset her, and she certainly didn't want the polish worn off the silver feeling she'd had since she'd met Parker. "I'll talk to him."

He frowned at the tightness in her voice. "I'm trying to help, not tell you what to do."

"I know."

Their gazes clung to each other, gauging the tense feeling. Finally Parker nodded. "All right. Thanks again for everything."

She waved as he pulled down the lane leading out to the road, very aware that, in spite of all the good feelings she'd had about their meeting, some of the magic had just slipped away.

"A BALL!" Hattie exclaimed that evening when Noreen finally told them about Parker's invitation. She'd spent hours mulling over it before opting for bravery. It was just a date.

"How wonderful, Noreen!" Charlene's face glowed.

Noreen put away the last of the supper plates. "It certainly sounds it, but I'm not sure I should go."

"Why not?" her three relatives chorused.

"I don't know." She shrugged as if her not going

was no big deal. To throw them off the track, she voiced the least of her worries. "I don't have anything to wear to something like that."

"We could do a fast shopping trip," Charlene suggested. "I like shopping."

"I don't know." Noreen sighed, crossing her arms as she stared out the window toward the pumpkin patch. "It's a lot of money to spend for a dress I'll only wear once. And I'm never very comfortable at functions like that."

"You would be, with Parker," Hattie said confidently. "Oh, do say you'll go, Noreen. It'll give us something to look forward to. We do so like that boy."

Noreen smiled at them, her expression indulgent. "I could tell. I almost think you put a spell on his car so he'd have to stay longer."

"Um, well, there's no need to worry about fitting in and doing Parker proud," Hattie said, averting the subject of cars. "You're a Cartwright, and on the same social footing as anyone else."

"Oh, I'd never fit in the city. I'm a country girl at heart."

"Yes, and you might as well not sit around and vegetate with the three of us when you have a chance to see the world," Priscilla said. "Even if it's only Dallas."

"I'll think about it." Noreen caught a glimpse of her stepbrother walking toward the house. "Right now, I have to talk to Garrison." She strode from the kitchen, determined to waylay him before he made it inside. It was high time she and he came to an understanding.

"WHAT DO YOU SUPPOSE that's all about?" Hattie shamelessly spied out the window, watching Garrison and Noreen both gesturing toward the house angrily.

"Noreen's giving him what for," Priscilla guessed. "Something I'm proud to see her finally doing."

"Oh, dear. I do want those two to get along," Charlene fretted.

"Impossible," Priscilla observed. "Garrison is a terminally ineligible bachelor and a weak excuse for a man. He has no job, and no concept of stability. He was a royal pain the entire time Parker was here. Anything Noreen's dishing out to him, he has coming."

"I agree. We have to do something about him." Though she appeared lighthearted, Hattie worried a lot about Noreen's future. She had three people on her side now but they were elderly, and none of them were up to sparring. If anything should happen to them, one day Noreen might be at Garrison's mercy. The will stipulated that the remaining six percent would be split evenly between the children at the aunts' passing. Hattie couldn't bear to think about it. "Maybe we're trying too hard to marry Noreen off. Maybe the one we should marry off is Garrison!" she said on a burst of inspiration. "He just needs a woman to keep him in line!" She looked to her sisters for confirmation of her brilliance.

"No one would have him," Priscilla said sourly. "He's such a weenie."

"Sister!" Charlene's jaw hung slack. "What would Pastor Jenkins say?"

"That no one would marry Garrison, either, I'm sure." Priscilla shook her head. "I said we'd rue the day my son married that woman—"

"Shh! No use crying over that now." Hattie tapped

her mouth with her finger. "Foisting Garrison off on some unsuspecting girl is probably the easy part, but we'll let Noreen handle him for now. The immediate emergency is getting her into a suitable ball gown."

They all considered that with pensive faces.

"I have several lovely gowns in my closet," Priscilla offered. "Any of them could be appropriate for this occasion, and I'm almost as tall as Noreen so the fit would be right."

"The vintage look is in," Hattie mused.

"Low heels and nobody would know the difference," Charlene added, still on dress length.

"No," Hattie said decisively. "She must wear high heels. Our Noreen is stunning, and we mustn't have her dressing down. Oh, can't you see how wonderful they'd look walking in, so tall and beautiful the pair of them?"

Outside, Noreen shook her head as Garrison left her in a huff to come inside the house. "That discussion is over," Priscilla observed. "Can we tie him and stuff him in a storage shed until the next century?"

"No." The phone rang and Hattie went to pick it up, not noticing that someone picked up on another phone at the same time. "Hello, Parker!"

"Hi, Hattie. Is Noreen around?"

"She's out in the fields." Hattie wished Noreen had come in when her stepbrother had, but apparently she'd needed some time to herself. "Can I have her call you?"

"I'm someplace I can't be reached for the next few hours, but I thought I'd call and see if she'd decided to accept my invitation this weekend."

Hattie gulped. "Um, as a matter of fact, she's delighted to be going with you."

"Really?" His voice perked up instantly. "That's great! I won't be able to come out to get her because I'm picking up some customers at the airport who will be going with us. Please tell Noreen I'll have the Executive Limo Service pick her up at six-thirty Saturday night, would you, Hattie? It's a very reputable company that I've used quite often for clients. I'd rather get Noreen, but these customers are from Canada, and I feel better meeting them at the airport."

"Oh, a limo! Noreen won't mind at all." Hattie nearly clapped her hands with glee. "We'll have her there with bells on." She hung up, excitedly turning to face her sisters. "Let's go look through your dresses, Priscilla. We've got planning to do!"

"How, exactly, do you propose to make Noreen go if she doesn't want to?" Priscilla demanded.

Hattie pursed her lips. "Oh, pooh. She wants to go. She's just afraid to let herself like Parker. The weight of responsibility has kept her from enjoying life fully, so it's up to us to see that she has this one night of passion, er, romance."

Priscilla eyed her narrowly. "I hope you know what you're doing. We've warned you before about misfiring your magic wand."

"I know, I know." Hattie brushed all that aside. "You may have been the pretty one, Priscilla, but I got all the brains. And, may I add, the guts to *just do it,* as they say in the modern vernacular."

"Sister!" Charlene remonstrated weakly. "Perhaps that's not quite appropriate at this time."

"Never mind. We've got to conjure up dream duds out of Priscilla's rags for our foxy babe. She's got a coach to catch come Saturday. Come on!'' she said, hurrying upstairs.

GARRISON'S EARS RANG with the scolding Noreen had just given him in the front yard. How dare she! Fortunately, he'd just happened to overhear this interesting conversation. He hung up the phone stealthily, his mind working. Noreen had a date with Mr. Wonderful, did she? If she thought she was going to ride off into the sunset and leave him playing the beggarly brother for the rest of his life, she was sadly mistaken.

He opened the phone book, grinning when he found the advertisement for the Executive Limo Service. Dear Noreen. She wasn't always going to be the favored one.

Perhaps a small detour in her life would shake her independent attitude enough to make her realize how precarious the soil was under her feet.

Chapter Seven

Saturday night promised to be an evening of glitter and glamor, but Parker kept checking his watch. Though he was surrounded by beautiful people having a great time, he couldn't keep his mind off of Noreen. She should have arrived by now.

He hoped the limo wasn't caught in traffic or broken down—as his own car mysteriously had at Noreen's farm. He ignored the niggling worry that she might have changed her mind and decided not to come. There would be absolutely no discussion concerning her land tonight. It was a topic destined to draw fire from his spirited lady. Parker comforted himself that she hadn't yet realized he was on *her* side. Once she did, everything should proceed smooth as a ribbon between them.

NOREEN PAID little attention to the scenery as the limo wound its way into downtown Dallas. The city lights were pretty, but her mind was occupied with Parker. Hattie, Charlene and Priscilla had worked their magic on her, but she wished she hadn't allowed her sweet aunt to goad her into accepting Parker's invitation. She didn't know Parker well enough to mingle with his business associates, not to mention that the body-hugging black evening gown Priscilla had shoe-horned her into made her nervous. The gown was missing its back, Noreen had fruitlessly tried to point out, her flesh exposed to nearly her derriere.

"Nonsense," Hattie had interrupted, "You look *très élégante!*"

Charlene had pinned Noreen's blond hair up into a lovely hairdo from which tiny curls hung provocatively. This left Noreen's shoulders exposed, and Hattie hadn't allowed her to get a shawl.

"Nonsense! It's nearly one hundred degrees outside!" Clucking, she'd helped Noreen slip on wonderful, black-beaded high heels. They fit perfectly.

"There! I knew it the minute I saw those shoes!" Hattie crowed, standing back to examine the effect, smiling in happy triumph.

Noreen had seen the Neiman Marcus box Hattie discreetly shoved out of sight and realized at once that not everything she had on tonight was borrowed from Grandma Priscilla's heyday. Aunt Hattie had been shopping—and she hadn't spared any expense. Her heart had sunk as she'd realized what her sweet little family was up to: they were out to snare a man for her.

Noreen sighed, not about to rest her head against the seat back for fear of mussing Charlene's hard work. She simply wasn't in the market for a man. Her misery level elevated just thinking how much the dream shoes Hattie had chosen must have cost.

"This is it," the limo driver said. "Your destination."

Noreen waited until he opened the door, allowing him to take her hand to help her out. A neon-lit night club resonated with blaring music. "Are you sure?" she asked uncertainly. The Pet E Club didn't look like a place Parker would habit, and she wasn't dressed for dancing to punk rock music.

The chauffeur checked his card. "This is the address I was given by Mr. Parker Walden."

"This must be it, then." She gave the chauffeur a hesitant smile. "Thank you."

"My pleasure." He gave her a big-toothed grin and bowed. "Please let us know if we can be of service in the future."

"I will." She nodded at him, pleased and reassured by the appreciative gleam in the young driver's eyes. He got in the sleek car and drove away. With her last feeling of security disappearing into the twilight-soft distance, Noreen took a deep breath and forced the beautiful shoes Hattie had bought her to move toward the door of the club.

Inside, her mouth opened in wonder at the spiked hair and pierced-earringed body parts cavorting in the dense light. More than one partyer turned to give her an inquisitive stare. Uncomfortable, Noreen realized she was more out of place in her splendid gown than they were in their awful costumes—Cinderella in a bad dream instead of at the ball.

Before she could talk to the bald-on-one-side woman who was taking money at the door, she was stopped by an enormous bouncer. "Can I help you?"

Noreen forced a small smile to her lips. "I'm supposed to meet someone here." Desperately, she glanced around for Parker.

The bouncer scratched his face. "You probably will, but something tells me you've got the wrong address."

"I was just beginning to think that myself. The trouble is, I'm not really sure where I am, or where I'm supposed to be." Moreover, she didn't have the first idea how to get in touch with Parker.

His brow rose in obvious disbelief at her confusion. "Now look, we don't have drugs in this establishment," the bouncer said sternly. "So if you're an undercover cop, you can look all you like, but nobody gets anything past me." He thumped his big chest with pride. "You'll just be wasting your time."

Obviously he was proud of his clientele. Noreen saw no reason to explain that she'd have to be on drugs to allow anyone to insert an earring through her bottom lip. "Could I use your phone, please? I'll...call a cab." She was phoning Hattie, and her aunt could harangue Ned Adams to drive his taxi out to get her. He was probably sitting in Hattie's parlor drinking tea right now, while *she* was subjected to a most un-enchanted evening.

"Come on." He jerked his head toward the cashier's booth. "There's a phone in there."

Noreen followed, avoiding the staring rockers' gazes. Her chest tightened with the fish-out-of-water sensation. Picking up the phone indicated by the bouncer, she dialed home.

"Hello?" Hattie's pert voice birdcalled into the receiver.

"Aunt Hattie!" Noreen hissed.

"Noreen! Oh, how sweet of you to take time out of your wonderful evening to call. Are you having a splendid time, dear?"

"No! I'm stuck on the wrong planet—or in a haunted house! Please call Ned and either have him come get me, or recommend a reputable cab company in Dallas who can take me home!'' Her relatives couldn't make the distance into Dallas, and the limo company was likely too expensive to see her back to her farm.

"A haunted house?'' There was a frown in Hattie's voice. "You should be at the ball raising funds, dear, not cavorting at one of those, especially wearing such a lovely evening gown.''

Noreen sighed. "I know, Aunt Hattie.''

"Is Parker not there with you?''

She glanced out at the twisting, jerking dancers. "Something tells me he hasn't been to this particular establishment.''

"Oh, dear.'' The phone beeped and Hattie gasped. "Oh, heavens! There's that silly call-waiting thing. I just hate that rude noise, and I can never figure out how to do it properly. But it might be Parker...just a minute, Noreen. If I lose you, call back.''

"Wait a—'' But the phone was dead, leaving Noreen to tap her foot. The cashier gave her a stern eyeing.

"Noreen?'' Hattie's voice came back on the line like a miracle.

Noreen straightened. "Yes?''

"Parker wants to know where you are.''

"Where I—'' Noreen couldn't remember. She glanced at the grim-eyed cashier. "Where am I?''

"Oh, man. What did you smoke tonight?'' She flipped a matchbook at her.

Noreen took it gratefully, reading the black zig-zag letters in a frantic motion. "I'm at the Pet E Club, Aunt Hattie.''

"Pet E? What a strange name.''

"I know.'' It was a strange place, but she didn't

think that was a good thing to say right now. The bouncer had returned to stand beside the cashier. They both looked as though they might be about to ask her to sweep floors and scrub dishes if she used their phone much longer.

"Let me see if I can get this thing to switch over again so I can tell Parker."

Hattie disappeared and Noreen closed her eyes. Why had she ever allowed her family to talk her into this?

"Parker says the limo driver should have taken you to the Petroleum Club," Hattie informed her a second later. "He's on his way to get you."

"Oh, thank heavens!" She breathed a sigh of relief.

"You just sit down and relax. Be sure you still have some lipstick on. Don't chew it all off," Hattie warned her. "This is just a minor bump in the evening."

"Thanks, Aunt Hattie." She had to smile at her aunt's enthusiasm. "I feel better now."

"Of course you do. You're a Cartwright, and Cartwrights never break in bad times. We have composure, a family trait."

"Yes, Aunt Hattie." Her Cartwright composure had come close to evaporating, but now that she knew Parker was on the way, Noreen felt better. "Goodbye, and thanks." She hung up and faced the bouncer and disapproving cashier. "My ride should be here any moment."

"How about buying a drink in the meantime?" the bouncer hinted.

Obviously a man who meant to make some profit

off her misery. "I think I could do that," she murmured.

"Seat yourself at the bar," he said more cheerfully than before. "Our bartender'll fix you right up."

It was difficult sliding up onto a barstool in her skin-fitting dress with the missing back. Noreen felt more like she slithered up, and the dress back slithered down to regions she wouldn't want exposed in a place like this. Hattie's voice remonstrated with her gently to mind her posture, so Noreen sat straight and ordered a champagne cocktail, which made the bartender laugh.

"Fancy lady, fancy drink," he commented.

"I am not fancy," she disagreed. "It's all I know to order, unless you've got iced tea." Thank heavens she had watched all those old movies with her father, wherein the heroines almost always had their beaux get them a sophisticated-sounding drink.

"Hey." A man wearing a patch over one eye occupied the seat next to her. "I'm Sinbad," he told her.

She could well imagine. "I'm...Scheherazade."

"Scheherazade?"

She nodded and accepted her drink.

"Where's your seven veils?" He glanced behind her, surreptitiously, for the veils, but his eye bulged when he saw her back.

He'd had too much to drink, she decided, or the decorative eye patch slowed his reactions. "I gave them up." She turned toward him so that he couldn't stare down her low-backed dress.

"Why?"

"I'm a modern girl. I can tell stories without

them." She took a sip of her drink and decided she spoke the truth.

"Cool. Hate to cover up anything of yours with a veil, anyway." He shrugged and pointed to a guy who took the seat on her other side. "That's Ben Franklin."

She smiled reluctantly, wondering if she should change her alias to Martha Washington. "It's... electrifying to meet you."

"Ha-ha." Ben guffawed and moved a little closer. "What's a pretty lady like you doing in a place like this?"

Apparently, pick-up lines hadn't changed since the real Ben Franklin had been born. Her smile didn't waver as she took in his spiked dog collar and leather wrist bands. "Same thing as everybody else, I suppose. Waiting for the clock to strike midnight."

"Hey, I like you." Sinbad leaned over, trying to see down the back of her dress again. "You're—"

Suddenly, strong hands cupped her shoulders. Noreen straightened and held back a yelp.

"Are you all right?"

The sound of Parker's deep voice was more than welcome—and exciting. *Cartwright composure,* Hattie's voice reminded her.

She had a ready, easygoing smile in place as she turned to face Parker—but her resolve slid into her stomach as she met his gaze. This was her rescuer, her Prince Charming. Dressed in a formal tux, he stole her breath. Parker's light hazel eyes, set off sexily by the rich darkness of his hair and perfectly fitted tux, held her gaze as if to never let go.

"I'm fine. I was just sitting here enjoying a conversation with Sinbad and Ben Franklin." Sinbad muttered something and slunk away, but Noreen only noticed by chance.

"You look lovely," Parker said simply.

It was all she needed to hear—heartfelt honesty in the middle of a loud, noisy place. She gave him her most seductive smile. "You look quite handsome yourself."

He glanced around before his gaze returned to her. "Are you sure you're all right?"

"I'm fine." And it was true—now. Parker made her feel safe, protected. And Hattie had been right: tonight was going to be enchanting.

"Let me get you out of here." He tossed some money on the bar to cover Noreen's barely touched drink and helped her slide off the stool. His palm rested lightly, protectively at the small of her back against the bare skin she had worried about being exposed earlier. Noreen suddenly felt physical attraction stirring inside her. She'd never felt this way before, never wanted to.

"I don't know how the limo driver messed up the instructions. I was quite clear about the directions." He gave her a worried once-over glance as he seated her in his Mercedes. "I should have just picked you up at the farm myself."

"You had clients, and I didn't mind being chauffeured," she admitted with a smile.

He closed the door, going around to slide into the driver's seat. "I don't know what I would have done if something had happened to you, though I'm impressed with how you handled the situation."

"How little you know. I was actually shaking in my boots."

He gave her ankles a swift glance before starting

the car. "I don't believe it, but if you were, I can only offer you my sincerest apology. I promise you nothing else will go wrong tonight."

With an apologetic smile, he brushed his lips against her knuckles. Noreen smiled, too, but her smile masked sudden nervousness. Why did this man have to be the most wonderful man she had ever met? They had nothing in common!

"Where's Meg tonight?" she asked to assuage her shifting emotions.

"Staying the night with my ex-wife's folks."

Noreen's stomach tightened instantly. "Oh," she said carefully.

"We're very close." He checked traffic behind him in the rearview mirror before changing lanes. "They like to have Meg over on Saturday nights, and any other they can squeeze out of me." He smiled ruefully. "I'm lucky to have them here."

What had she gotten herself into? She didn't want to fall for a man whose ex-wife still held his affection! Desperately she searched her memory, trying to recall what he'd revealed about their relationship.

"Don't worry." He covered her hand with his own. "I may be very close to my in-laws, but neither they nor I see my ex very often."

"Poor Meg." Noreen's lashes dropped as she stared at the tiny beads shining on her dress. It couldn't be good for a little girl not to see her mother, no matter how adoring the father.

"She's doing okay. It would be better to have a family that all lived together, but Meg hasn't ever known anything else." He pulled up outside a tall, well-lit building that looked nothing like the other she'd visited tonight. "I'll let you out here and go park.'' He moved to open his door so that he could go around to let Noreen out, but she touched his wrist, halting him.

"I'll walk with you."

His gaze wandered slowly from her upswept hair down to her clinging gown. "Are you sure?"

"I'm positive."

"You're not worried about your hair or your shoes?"

"Charlene put enough pins in my hair to compete with this building for durability. Besides, I feel like walking.'' Truthfully, she wanted to spend every magical moment of this evening with him.

"You've got a deal.'' He gave her an admiring glance and drove into a space at the side of the building. Turning the car off, he said in a confiding, husky tone, "I'm really glad you could come tonight, Noreen."

It thrilled her to hear it. "So am I," she whispered, her voice tight with the excitement and wonder she felt.

They held each other's gaze for a moment. It was only a millisecond in reality, yet it was long enough for Noreen to know that her heart was in imminent danger of being stolen by the very man who had rescued her.

NOREEN WAS HAVING a lovely time, much better than she wanted to admit. Parker was an escort any woman would want—and obviously many women did. But he seemed to have eyes only for her, a fact which made her smile bright with happiness.

It was nearing midnight now. Parker had sent his out-of-town clients off to their hotel. "You've done your charitable duty for tonight. I know you've got to be up early, but if you've got an hour, I'd like to spend some time alone with you before I take you home.''

''I'd like that, too.''

He put his hand at the small of her back to guide her through the crowd to the door. A petite, older woman, overdressed in diamonds and stiff taffeta, stopped him with a hand on his arm.

''Parker Walden! I just heard you're expanding into East Texas.''

He appeared suddenly uncomfortable.

''Not so far east. Just looking around in Rockwall. Mrs. Balfour, I'd like you to meet Noreen Cartwright.''

''How nice to meet you, Noreen.'' She took in her gown with an approving glance before returning to her original mission. ''Parker, don't fend me off. If you've found property that will suit Balfour Investments, you need to let me in on it at once. We're going to be putting our clients somewhere in the next two weeks, and it might as well be Rockwall as the other side of Dallas.''

Parker was silent for a moment. *He's hedging,* Noreen knew instinctively.

He took a deep breath. ''My company *has* acquired a nice tract of acreage in Rockwall,'' he finally said. ''Call me Monday and I'll discuss the parameters with you.''

Mrs. Balfour beamed, patting Noreen on the arm. ''I knew if rumor had it Parker Walden was expanding his interests, it was likely true. Where there's smoke, there's fire, you know.'' She kissed his cheek. ''She's lovely, Parker. I'll call you. Good night.'' She gave them both a regal inclination of her head and departed.

For the first time that evening, Parker didn't look directly at her. Noreen's blood felt thin with inexplicable worry. "Parker," she said, touching her hand to his lapel so he'd stop propelling her forward. "You didn't tell me you'd acquired a property in Rockwall."

His face was grim. "I was going to tell you when we were alone."

"Oh?" A chilly sensation crept over her, making her stomach clench. "Should you tell me now?" Surely Garrison hadn't wheedled Parker into buying out his portion of Cinderella Acres! She'd have to sue her stepbrother for violating the terms of her father's will, and she didn't want to do that. It was imperative that she do everything she could to keep their relationship the way her father had hoped it would be—close.

Even if they weren't that way at all. But she couldn't bear to think how disappointed her father would be.

"Okay." Parker sighed heavily. "I bought the land behind yours."

"You did?" Relief swept her, before comprehension dawned. "But you said that my land was zoned residential. You wouldn't be interested in that kind of real estate."

"It is." He stared down at her. "But I learned that the land behind you was zoned for either."

Visions of garish billboards behind her family's homes instantly swam through her mind. She shook her head in dazed confusion.

Running a hand through hair that hadn't been out

of place all night, he said, "Noreen, they were going to sell to someone. Commercial ventures are my business."

"I know, but..." She fought against the fear she knew was irrational—and the disappointment. Her distrust of real estate developers was ingrained. She could fight against anyone but Parker.... Had her trust been misplaced? She searched his eyes for understanding. There was nothing emotional there that she could see. Noreen wanted desperately to know that she and her family were more important to him than putting fast-food eateries and maybe a huge movie complex with fifty screens right at her door. The price of her land would skyrocket, but her way of life would be numbering its days to extinction. "Farming is *my* business, Parker."

And she was the very one who had suggested he look at that land! Had she lost her mind? She hadn't known he was such a successful developer, then, one who was on cheek-kissing terms with the elite in the business. Her only thought had been for poor Mrs. Martin who had lost her husband and who needed a quick buyer. Parker's appearance had seemed like fate, not threatening to Noreen in any way.

But that was before I knew I cared for him, she thought miserably. *That was when it was just any old Sunday afternoon—not the rest of my life.*

In the crowd someone's watch beeped the hour. *Probably belongs to a young, slick, new kid on the block who doesn't have an expensive Rolex like Parker's,* Noreen thought disjointedly.

It was midnight, and her hero had turned into someone she was afraid to trust.

Chapter Eight

"Let's talk about this at my house." Parker took Noreen by her arm and pulled her away from the crush of people, drawing her outside.

"Wait." She pulled back, and he released her instantly. "I...I'm not sure that I should.... Maybe it's best if you just take me home."

He frowned, his brows pulling together in a dark line. "Noreen, I think you should give me a chance to explain."

"Maybe I should, but..." She searched his eyes worriedly. "Can't you explain on the way back to my farm?"

Hesitating a moment, he put his hand out to catch hers. His skin was warm and sinfully inviting against hers. "Is that really the way you want it?"

She was silent, afraid to answer. It wasn't the way she wanted the evening to end, and he knew it. But there was too much risk in allowing herself to fall any deeper under this man's spell. They had far too much keeping them apart, and the sting of betrayal she felt at learning of his development deal wasn't going to go away easily.

"It isn't the way *I* want it," he said softly, his tone compelling.

She lowered her gaze, pressing her lips together in indecision. His hand still held hers, and Noreen could feel the subtle pull of attraction between them. "You can't have everything you want," she told him, knowing it was a spiteful comment and not feeling good about it. Anything to keep temptation at bay!

"No." Sensing her hesitation, he tugged her hand until she was forced to stand close to him. Winding an arm around her so that she fit snugly up under the rougher texture of his tux jacket, Parker placed a gentle kiss on her lips. "Rarely have I wanted anything as much as I want you, though."

How could she say no to Parker wanting her? No man had ever said anything like that to her! Noreen slowly forced her eyelashes upward so that their gazes met. "I don't know what to say."

"Say yes," he murmured, his lips nuzzling against hers. "Just for an hour."

An hour, she told herself. What harm could there be in that? Sixty minutes to talk and hear his plans for the land he'd bought. Two half hours in the company of a dynamic man she admired, though she tried hard not to.

"Yes," she said finally, throwing caution to the wind.

AT THE FARM Garrison rolled his eyes at the little old ladies sitting around playing cards with Ned Adams. Card games were for the weak of mind! There were so much more interesting games to play. He frowned to himself. Of course, the fact that his beloved Ferrari was going to be repossessed in a week wasn't a game, as the phone call he'd taken today attested. Being dunned by the bank had him in a royal snit.

It's all their fault. His eyes narrowed as he watched Hattie, Charlene and Priscilla get up to answer the door. *And Noreen's.* How silly they all were, their lives so simple and unintelligent.

"Dixie! Come in!" Hattie kissed her cheek, and they exchanged warm hugs, but he couldn't see the face of the surprise card-party crasher. "How kind of you to come by! Garrison, come say hello to Dixie, Ned's granddaughter!"

He straightened reluctantly. No relation of the taxi driver's could remotely interest him.

Dixie walked in, and Garrison's jaw fell open.

She was a living doll.

Not his type, of course, with those sugary freckles and that bronze hair. Not his type, because he preferred long-limbed women who looked great in Kamali swimwear. This little bit of a girl was almost flat-chested with an athlete's body and good country health shining from every pore. Absolutely zero to put in a D-cup. But as he reached to take her hand in his, Garrison felt his heart doing a slow tattoo of dawning excitement. "Hello, Dixie."

"Hi!" She gave him a pert smile, showing tiny white teeth that were dentist perfect.

"Hey, Garrison," Ned called. "Whatsa matter wichya? You look peaked suddenly, son." The older man shuffled cards with a dry look his way.

"I feel fine…sir." Garrison purposely tagged the respectful title on for effect. Remembering to release Dixie's hand, Garrison stepped back a pace or two. Dixie watched him with considering, large blue eyes.

"This time, me and Ned'll play against Charlene

and Priscilla," Hattie said confidently. "Garrison, unless you want to watch us old folks play cards, why don't you and Dixie go into town to get a soda or something?"

He shook his head immediately. No way. He wasn't getting in a car with her! Conversation would be too difficult with a woman so definitively not his type.

"Come on." Dixie gently socked him on the upper arm. "You look like you could use some caffeine in your blood. I'll drive Grandpa's truck, if you're not feeling well enough to drive."

"Truck?" He hadn't ridden in one of those contraptions in years. They weren't his style.

"I rode over on my motorcycle." Dixie shrugged. "Grandpa doesn't mind me borrowing his truck, though."

He realized he was gaping at her, before his glance took in his reproving relations. Okay, so his bad manners were showing. Why did *he* have to get stuck entertaining Ned's granddaughter?

"All right," he said reluctantly. "You can drive." It would never do for him to be seen with this woman in his Ferrari at the local Sonic drive-in. He had a reputation to uphold, and he wasn't about to be seen with a cab driver's family member in his expensive car. Maybe if they went in her grandfather's truck, they wouldn't stand out as much, and no one would recognize him.

He refused to think about the motorcycle this woman apparently used for transportation.

"Take good care of him, Dix," Ned called.

"I will, Grandpa."

They waved and went out. He was so rattled by

the lovely pear shape of Dixie's backside as she swished past him that Garrison only just remembered to open the door for her.

"Completely flummoxed," Hattie said with satisfaction when they'd gone.

"Bamboozled," Charlene agreed.

"I never would have believed Garrison could be so...well, caught off guard," Priscilla said. "You didn't tell us your Dixie was such a package of dynamite, Ned."

He grinned. "Runs in the family," he said, winking at Hattie.

She appeared to ignore his remark. "I did tell all of you that Garrison needed a woman to divert him from his own selfishness," she reminded them, sticking to safer ground. "It's him we ought to have been working on marrying off all along. That would solve *all* of our problems."

Ned scratched his head. "I still think if there's going to be a wedding around here, it oughta be me and you, Hattie."

"That wouldn't solve *any* of our problems." She tapped him smartly on the arm with her cards.

Charlene raised her brows. "What makes you think that Dixie would have a weenie like Garrison, Hattie?"

"Charlene!" The smile slid right off Hattie's face in shock at her gentle sister's choice of language. Worse, though, was the realization that the entire group was staring expectantly at Hattie as if she would have an answer to the question Charlene posed.

"Well, that's what Priscilla calls him," Charlene said defensively, "and you know Dixie's got way too much common sense to fall for such a selfish airhead as that boy. Some things are impossible, even for you, Hattie.''

"She's got a point," Ned commented.

"Oh, hush." Hattie was becoming cross, and the cards in her hand didn't make her feel any better. "Well, maybe Dixie wouldn't want a weenie for a husband," she allowed, her tone defeated. Then her positive attitude rescued her. "But at least our Noreen is having a wonderful time tonight."

"Except for the little detour to the punk rock club," Priscilla reminded her.

"That was just a teeny little misfortune in the evening." Hattie's good humor intensified. "For the first time, both of our responsibilities are out with suitable dates and having the times of their lives," she sang out with enthusiasm. "It all gets better from here, I can just feel it in my bones!"

GARRISON BUMPED ALONG in the truck, his ears pierced by the squawking of the crated chickens in the pickup bed. Hay flew up his nose and stung his eyes. He sneezed uncontrollably.

Dixie seemed not to notice as she parked in a middle spot at the well-lit drive-in, jamming the brake on firmly enough to make a crate slide forward with a loud bang. Garrison set his teeth.

"Here we are!"

She looked at him with the most adorable smile he'd ever seen. Even through the allergic watering of his eyes he could see the dimple highlighting her sweet smile. "Yeah, here we are," he replied with a disdainful sniff.

"What do you want?"

A tissue to blow his nose in, and the hay fever

attack to go away. Mostly, he wanted the cheerleader in the truck from hell to take him back home. Their hellmobile with its squawking chickens was attracting stares and laughter from surrounding cars. Garrison picked a piece of chaff off his once-perfectly clean cotton shirt. "Nothing."

"Oh, come on." She gave him a smile that almost melted his heart, but Garrison withstood it. "You need something to wash down a hay fever capsule." She pulled a small box from her purse, offering it to him.

"You carry allergy pills on you?" She didn't seem the type that anything could affect negatively.

"Well, sure! I'm a farmer, you know." She pushed the box into his hands. "I'd be dying all the time from my allergies if I didn't take something for it."

He pushed a pill out of the foil while she ordered drinks for them. It was nice that they had something in common, even if it was only hay fever.

The problem was what she had just told him. She was a farmer, and the last woman he'd ever be attracted to was one who made her living from the ground. He'd had enough of that for a lifetime! Farming didn't pay for Ferraris and Egyptian cotton shirts.

But all this sneezing had reminded him about his mission: he had to get rid of the land he owned. Country air and vegetation wasn't healthy for him. But to do that, he needed a real estate broker who specialized in country land tracts. If Parker wasn't interested in his property, then he'd find a broker who was.

"Here." Dixie handed him a drink.

Belatedly he realized that the car hop needed to be paid. He pulled money from his wallet with one hand, juggling the pills he hadn't taken and the drink with the other. The transaction completed, he swallowed the medicine, blew his nose on a rough napkin printed with red letters and smiled confidently at Dixie. "Guess you noticed that the land behind ours was for sale."

She cocked her head. "Actually, I heard Grandpa say that some guy from Dallas bought it."

"Really?" This was the best news Garrison had heard in a long time. "Wonder who it was?"

"I don't know." She shrugged, digging into some potato tots covered with cheese which looked disgusting to Garrison. "But he had to outbid another party for it. The price went really high."

"You don't say." Garrison stiffened, not noticing the interested stares at the hellmobile now. A bidding war meant that the person who lost out might be very interested in *his* property!

"Yep," Dixie said. "Want a tater tot?"

He shook his head at her offer. "No, thanks. I wish I knew who had bought that land," he murmured.

"Well, I don't know that, but I do know who got outbid. It was Crower Real Estate in Dallas."

"*Crower?*" They were the biggest developers in Texas! His heart beat like he was running a race. "How could they get outbid?"

She shrugged. "Don't know. I heard Grandpa say something about a handshake of honor between the buyer and the seller. But there's some bad blood between the two bidders now. Guess Crower wasn't too happy to lose."

That meant Crower Real Estate might very likely be interested in what he wanted to sell. "Gee, Dixie, I didn't think you and I would have much to talk about, but you're a veritable font of information."

She paused, her fork to her lips. "You know, I'm not so sure you're not weird. Cute, but weird."

That hurt. "I'm not weird!"

"I'm pretty sure you are," she disagreed. "It's like, here I am telling you this story about these poor people who had to sell their land, and you don't care about them. You just care about what that's going to do to the price of where your fancy duds are hanging."

"They wanted to sell, didn't they?"

"Only because the husband had died and the wife couldn't keep her farm up anymore. Couldn't pay the death taxes on it, for that matter." Dixie gave him a belligerent stare.

"Well, she doesn't have to worry about money now," he pointed out reasonably.

"She'd rather have her husband back, and their way of life!"

"I'd rather have the money." He shrugged at her astonishment. "I'm sorry if that offends you, but there's nothing comparable to being able to pay the bills."

"You have a cold heart." She rested her drink between her thighs, which made him think about parts of her body he shouldn't wonder about. "I'd better take you home."

Suddenly, it hit him that he didn't want her disapproving of him this much. He'd never been unceremoniously taken home, as if he were a bad schoolboy. The women he dated were more than content to stay out all night with him.

As long as he was spending money, he realized. He hadn't minded.

But now he sat in a small-town drive-through in a

squawking road-worn truck with a petite-breasted, short-legged woman who'd only cost him about three bucks for the evening, and who wanted him to be sad for a widow he'd met once in his entire life.

The effects of the hay fever tablets must be making me dopey, Garrison thought disjointedly, *because suddenly, I see her point.*

But he didn't want to. "Are you taking me home or not?" he demanded briskly.

"You'd better believe I am," she retorted, her blue eyes frosty above her perky little nose.

Good, he told himself. *The last thing I need is little Miss Hay Fever giving me sermons about life. She's a bossy, lippy woman, not my type at all.*

She had such pretty lips, though....

"Can't this bucket of bolts go any faster?" he demanded as she pulled up onto the gravel-rimmed road.

"Nope. Not unless I want to wreck."

The road curved nicely into the dark. Parker sighed to himself, glad that he'd quit sneezing. Now he just felt drowsy. He leaned his head against the seat back. "I don't want you to wreck."

"I'm surprised. I can't imagine you'd be concerned for my well-being."

"I'm concerned for mine," he said, glancing over at Dixie's pretty bronze ponytail blowing in the breeze. He wouldn't want anything to happen to her, either, but he wasn't about to flatter bossy, lippy Miss Hay Fever with his momentary emotion.

It would pass. He'd make it pass.

NOREEN WASN'T SURPRISED by the beauty of Parker's home. The man had acquired the best of everything, including land. She felt encroached upon.

Silently he walked into the living room where she was awkwardly perched on a wing chair. He handed her the glass of ginger ale she'd requested. She wasn't about to take the chance of softening under a wine-induced, romantic haze.

"Thank you." The cold of the glass steadied the nervousness she felt inside.

"You're welcome. Ginger ale sounded good to me, too." He raised his glass to her. "To a beautiful lady."

Her face froze like the ice in her drink. She couldn't smile, or think of the right reply. She was too upset. "Parker, what are you going to do with that acreage?"

"I like a woman who gets right to the point." He sat in the wing chair opposite hers and stared into the marble-treated fireplace the chairs framed. "Truthfully, that depends a lot on you."

"Me!"

"Yeah." He didn't meet her gaze. "I bought it so no one else could get near you."

Her throat dried out. "What are you saying?" she whispered.

"I think I'm falling for you, Noreen."

His voice was a rasp that stole her breath. She stared at him.

"I haven't liked a woman in a long time." He grimaced, as if admitting that he did now was painful. "My ex-wife was fond of telling me that I was no fun. That I was uptight. We didn't suit, I can see now, but when I fell in love with her, I couldn't imagine that there were any boundaries between us that love couldn't overcome.''

"I know what you mean." Noreen stared into the fizzy bubbles rising in her ginger ale. Common sense told her that she and Parker didn't suit. Her long-denied heart insisted that love was enough. But she had to be more practical than that. She had a family to support and a farm to get in the black. Falling in love foolishly had never been a luxury she could afford.

"I suppose I do work too much. I probably am an overachiever." He shrugged and reached to loosen his tie. "Maybe that translates into uptightness."

"Or success."

"My marriage certainly wasn't successful. So I guess I've resisted a second serious relationship." His gaze, when he turned it toward her, was piercingly honest.

"I don't really see what's wrong with being driven. I'm driven, too," Noreen admitted. "Nobody's going to be happier than me if my pumpkin crop turns out to be the bonanza it promises. I stare out at those vines day and night, wondering, visualizing, wanting. Sometimes I think the wait will kill me." She smoothed a nervous hand through her upswept tresses. "So I must be uptight, too. It probably means we wouldn't suit. I've always heard opposites attract, and obviously, we're alike."

"I've always heard likes stay together." He sighed deeply. "Noreen, I sense the wall you put up between us. From the first time I met you, I felt your reluctance. What is it?"

"Your livelihood." It was hard saying it, but he deserved the truth. "Your way of life is different from mine. You're city, I'm country. You sell and develop land, I want to nurture it.'' Carefully she set her drink on the tiny Chinese table next to her. ''Parker, I don't understand what you mean by saying that what you do with that land depends on me.''

''Would you marry me?''

''*What?*'' Noreen's jaw dropped. Parker didn't blink as he calmly said the words a woman dreams of hearing—from the right man. How could he sit there so calmly, when she was afraid she hadn't heard him right?

''I want to know if you'll marry me.''

She'd heard him right, but it was the last thing she ever dreamed he'd say.

But he said it so...emotionlessly. Almost as if...it was just another business deal.

And then it hit her. ''Does my answer affect what happens to your recent acquisition?''

He pressed his lips together with displeasure. ''Noreen, I'm not trying to bribe you, if that's what you're asking.''

Her spine unkinked a bit. She smoothed her long skirt with fingers that searched for something to do. ''Then quit toying with me. Tell me exactly what's on your mind!''

''Do you have an answer to *my* question?'' One dark brow lifted in inquiry.

''Parker, I can't marry you! I can hardly take a marriage proposal from you seriously, after the conversation we just had about...well, your previous marriage. You said you and your ex-wife didn't suit. It's a given that you and I don't, either.''

''In some ways, no. In the ways that count, I think we might.'' He ran a hand through his hair, sending the dark spikes into disarray. "I didn't mean to throw my proposal out so awkwardly. I'm sorry."

She leaned back, a little more soothed that he didn't seem upset by her negative answer. "For some reason, I'm sorry, too."

"You don't have anything to apologize for."

"Well, for my reaction. I wasn't expecting a marriage proposal tonight." She circled her fingers around the cold glass on the table to center herself. "It was nice, in a way."

He gave her a deprecating smile. "Meg likes you, you know."

Her skin chilled. "I like her, too. Is that what this is about? A stepmother for your daughter?"

"In part," he admitted. "I'd like a whole family for her."

"I...see." Her heart curled in disappointment. *Falling for you, not necessarily falling in love with you, silly,* a chiding voice berated her. *You were thinking about protecting your farm, and he was thinking about his family.*

It was sobering, and made her feel selfish. "Meg is a wonderful child, Parker." She moved to sit at his knees where she could take his hand and stare up into his eyes. "She deserves a whole family," she said softly. "I'm flattered you'd consider me. I could easily love her as my very own."

"You could?" His voice was hoarse, hopeful.

A wistful smile touched Noreen's lips. "Of course. Who would not love that child? She is precious, adorable. My aunts and grandmother have absolutely flipped over her. They were hoping you'd let them watch her next weekend."

"I'd like for Meg to experience all the love that's

in your home, Noreen.'' Parker allowed Noreen to take his fingers tighter in hers. ''It's everything a man wants for his little girl. A wonderful place in the country where she can run and play to her heart's content. Flowers, horses, fresh air. A loving, built-in family.'' He paused. The pain in his eyes nearly broke Noreen's heart. ''I thought buying that land next to yours...well, I thought it would make a nice wedding gift.''

''Wedding gift?'' Noreen's eyes widened. She'd been imagining malls and movieplexes! The man wanted to give her the moon on a platter—albeit to achieve his dream—and she'd suspected him of money-mongering motives. ''Oh, Parker, I can't believe— Oh, dear.'' Her eyes filled with sudden, irritating tears. He pulled her up into his lap, and Noreen was more than glad to rest her head against his chest. ''What a prince of a man you are.''

''Not really,'' he said gruffly. ''You see I had an agenda.''

''I know. But a nice one.'' She sniffled, running a finger under her bottom lashes to catch the moisture.

''Well,'' he said on a heavy sigh. ''I suppose it's true that money can't buy love.''

''Or a mother for your child,'' Noreen said quietly. ''Parker, the right woman is out there, who will love you for you and be glad Meg is the icing on the cake.''

''I don't like dating because of Meg,'' he said ruefully. ''Every woman I meet, I think about Meg. A bachelor can find a woman easily enough, but it's not the same for a father. The right woman is harder to find. And I've already married the wrong woman once.'' He gently turned her head so that she stared down into his eyes. "When I met you, something told me you had it all," he said huskily. "A dream woman, with everything I was looking for."

"I'm flattered, Parker. I wish I could be her," Noreen whispered, her heart torn. What woman wouldn't love Meg for a daughter, wouldn't thrill to the compliment that Parker was honoring her with? But, as gently and tempting as he'd presented it, Parker was only making a business deal—and both of them knew it. "You make me feel like Cinderella, standing on the verge of dream-come-true land."

He reached to frame her face with one palm. "Cinderella just needed a chance, the right opportunity," he said, never taking his eyes from hers. "Maybe I'm the Cinderella of this story." He touched his lips to hers, hovering as he waited for her reaction. Noreen felt him touch her hair. Pin by pin, the glorious hairdo gave way to his fingers. "Maybe I just need a chance with you," he murmured.

"Fairy tales are supposed to have happy endings," she softly rebutted, tingling all over as he brushed his fingers against her cheek, then sifted through the long hair he'd undone.

He kissed up her neck to her lips, hovering. "This one might yet."

Chapter Nine

"I'd like to believe that there could be a happy ending for us." She was mesmerized by the stroking pull of his fingers in her hair. In the dimmed light their world seemed small, enclosing the two of them in a private place nothing could intrude upon. She felt safe, wanted. "I think my farm roots may be too much to overcome, though," she whispered.

"Noreen, my business isn't exactly synonymous with the devil's work."

That made her smile. "No, I meant I'm always looking for the other shoe to drop. Everything can be going along fine with the crops, but I can't help looking for the disaster that will destroy my dreams. I know it sounds pessimistic, but it's ingrained in me. Reality for me is hard winds, too much sun, too little sun, no rain...."

"I get it." He sighed, moving his hand from her hair so that it rested in a comforting way against her neck. "I don't think there is another shoe where we're concerned, Noreen."

"Maybe not." They sat together, resting their heads against each other, in front of the pretty fireplace that held a bouquet of silk flowers in its opening. It all felt too good, too right. She wanted to let herself fall, go headlong into the dream.

But something told her that anything that felt this perfect wasn't going to have a happy ending.

AT CINDERELLA ACRES the card-playing foursome put away their cards. "We'd best get home, ladies," Hattie said. "I can tell it's going to be a late night. We don't want to embarrass Noreen by the hour at which she returns."

"I agree." Priscilla stood. "Some things are not our business."

"Well, we can call the evening a success," Charlene said in her happily satisfied tone. "Since Noreen didn't come home early, she's obviously having the time of her life. Something we were too afraid to really believe might happen."

"Exactly." Hattie nodded her agreement. "Our part is done. Come on, old man, drive us home." She put out her hand to Ned, who took it immediately to help her up out of the chair. "Too bad Dixie didn't have as good a time with Garrison."

Dixie had left on her motorcycle after her and Garrison's drive into town. Hattie had noticed neither party appeared too happy with the other. *One case where my wand went awry,* she thought with a shrug, but she was allowed a mistake when the raw material was lacking. Garrison *was* a weenie, though she had never spoken such aloud to her sisters. To do so would be to agree with them, confirming the truth about the boy. Even ever-optimistic Charlene had thrown in the towel on him. Yet, somehow she just *knew* there had to be some good in him!

But he'd had that bad seed of a mother...the

one who'd wanted the farm. She forced that worrisome thought away.

"We'll all pile into your truck, Ned, or you can walk us home. But it'd save you a trip walking back over here." She waited for her sisters and Ned to reply. Ned's truck was no carriage, and one of them would have to ride in the back.

"No point in him having to walk back. Lock up, Hattie." Priscilla turned off lights, leaving a small lamp on for Noreen. "I've ridden with chickens before. Let's just get going."

"If you ladies don't mind the vehicle." Ned's weathered face looked worried.

"We don't. Come on, Ned." Charlene ushered him out the door. "We're farm girls."

Hattie looped her arm through his after she locked the front door. He gallantly helped the other two sisters with his free hand to step off the porch, then escorted her to slide onto the bench seat. Ned was such a gentleman. It was a shame she couldn't accept his proposal. But she had things on her mind, matters that needed to be accomplished which might not be tended to as well if she were trying to be a new bride.

He helped Charlene in next to Hattie, then went around to drop the truck gate so Priscilla could slide up on it.

"Hang on tight," Hattie heard him tell her. "I'll drive real slow and careful."

"Don't mind me, Ned Adams," Priscilla shot back. "I'm not going to break riding from here to my house. Don't treat me like an old lady!"

Hattie smiled to herself. None of them were old, really. They were energetic and useful! There'd be even more to do if Noreen snagged that city boy. A little girl would come to live at Cinderella Acres....

Hattie closed her eyes and dreamed. Wished hard. When she opened her eyes, she saw a shooting star flame white across the velvet sky. A great-goddaughter! A great-grandniece of her own. A little girl, a miracle she'd never allowed herself to hope for. Never really thought she'd be lucky enough to have in this life, with Noreen not being partial to manhunting.

Ned got in beside her, starting the truck. Slowly he started toward the three little houses, ever so mindful of the rutted well-driven path between Noreen's house and theirs. Of course he need not drive so slow, even though Priscilla was dangling her legs from the tailgate. Sister was tougher than that! But she smiled to herself when Ned twined his rough fingers through hers and settled their hands on his jean-covered thigh. He was a good man.

She wanted the very same kind of man for Noreen.

She closed her eyes again. *Maybe tonight is the night those two will realize they're perfect for each other. I've never wasted my wishes in my whole life.*

Please let me have this one. I'll love Meg so much.

PARKER AWAKENED with a start, noting by his watch that it was 3:00 a.m. Noreen had slid down into his lap, resting her head against his chest so that she slept deeply. She'd even kicked off her shoes. He leaned his head against the wing chair, trying to decide what to do with this beautiful woman. The right thing would be to wake her up and take her home. Her relatives had to be worried sick, not to mention they no doubt thought he was taking advantage of Noreen.

He smiled as she shifted and slipped one hand around his torso. This lady didn't know it, but she was well on the way to sneaking into a place in his heart he'd never want her to leave. He hadn't been kidding when he'd told her she was everything he'd ever wanted in a woman. More than that, she was "just right" for Meg, too. The three of them would fit together like spokes on a wheel, regardless of Noreen's wary nature. But he understood her reluctance to fall into a relationship with him. She was being practical. He actually liked her more for her approach, because it won his trust. If she'd fallen all over him, she would have been so much like the other women who only wanted to be seen with him for his social connections or his money. Of all the women he'd known, Noreen probably had more need of money than anyone else. Yet she had refused his marriage proposal without a blink.

If he ever convinced Noreen to say yes, it would be because she was in love with him. That was a happy ending he wanted more than anything.

For him *and* for Meg.

NOREEN AWAKENED in a big bed, curled next to Parker's hard body as if she'd spent the night with him many times before. Her eyes flew open in slight alarm, before she realized that she still had her evening gown on, and he was sleeping in his tux shirt and trousers.

Somehow, she was extremely comfortable. He had one hand resting in the curve of her hip, and his face buried in her hair. One leg rested between hers, allowed access by the back slit of her gown. She smiled, deciding she liked the intimacy. The lighted digital clock on the bedside table glowed 6:00 a.m. Though she was usually at work by now, Noreen closed her eyes, allowing herself to enjoy the dream a little while longer.

GARRISON got into his Ferrari, humming as he drove away from the farm. How nice it was to be in his own sleek vehicle, rather than the hellmobile from last night! It had taken hours for his nose to unclog sufficiently for him to sleep, and he was certain his ears would ring awhile longer—either from the chicken symphony or the cold tablets Dixie had probably poisoned him with.

But she'd been good for one thing: she'd been a compass pointing him in the right direction. Crower Real Estate would likely be very interested in the land he had to sell.

"And then you'll be all mine," he told the Ferrari. "No more irritating bankers calling to repossess you."

Dixie would laugh at his obsession with his dream car. To Ned and Dixie Adams, a car was a convenience, not a comfort. It didn't matter if they drove trucks or motorcycles, as long as it had wheels and an engine and got them where they and their chickens needed to go.

That wasn't good enough for Garrison Cartwright. He needed expensive leather and luxury appointments.

He caught the unusual hitch in the car's smooth acceleration as he headed onto the farm road which ran through town. Frowning, he dismissed it. The Ferrari hadn't given him an ounce of trouble before. She was like the woman of his dreams: she did everything he wanted her to do, he thought smugly.

Suddenly "she" stopped cold. He barely had time to jerk the wheel to the right so that he could coast over the line onto the soft shoulder of the road.

"What are you doing?" he demanded of the car. "What the devil is wrong with you?" He tried to start it again. It gave a throaty cough but declined to come to life. "Oh, please," he begged it, the same way he would anyone else from whom he wanted something. "I've got a mission today, which is to keep you in my name." The car ignored him and sat in the summer heat, obviously not going another mile without assistance.

Garrison scratched his head. The car was new! Well, only a few years old, but he never told anyone that. He'd bought it from a car salesman and gambling buddy of his who only sold the best used vehicles. So why in the world would it act this way? His buddy had assured him that this dream machine would hardly ever need much more than oil in its life. Getting out of the car, he stood in the sun staring at the beautiful fire color and sleek lines of the only thing he'd ever wanted with a passion.

He wanted to cry.

Dusty gravel suddenly sprayed near his Italian snakeskin loafers.

"Car trouble, Garrison?"

His eyes fairly popped at the sight of the last person on earth he wanted to see. "Uh, no, Dixie," he lied. "Everything is fine."

"Then why are you sitting there like your horse died?" She pulled off her helmet, and the bronze ponytail caught the sunlight. Her pixie smile was teasing, her voice too polite.

Darn her, anyway.

"The stupid thing stalled, and I have no idea why," he replied, knowing he sounded churlish.

"Gee, that's too bad. Maybe you should think about becoming a mechanic if you're going to drive those expensive buggies." She snapped her helmet back on. "Well, gotta run. See ya."

With a crescendo of the motorcycle engine, she pulled up onto the highway and sped off. The witch! He fumed, knowing she hadn't offered him assistance on purpose. She was laughing at him! Just because he hadn't been overly appreciative of the merits of her grandfather's hell-roadster. Thousands of dollars sitting by the roadside useless, and she'd barely been able to contain her giggle and the glee in her sparkling blue eyes.

Suddenly, the motorcycle roared back to the Ferrari again. Garrison rolled his eyes. Ha! The woman wasn't immune to him after all.

"Maybe someone oughta look at your car," she suggested.

"Oh, do you think so?" he commented sarcastically.

"Yes, I do." She smiled at him with those full lips and straight, white teeth, like she had the world by the tail. "A phone call for a wrecker might be the best place to start. Unless you have a roadside assistance plan that serves rural areas."

He ground his teeth. "Not at the moment." It would take hours to get someone to come out from Dallas.

"Oh, brother," she sighed. "Well, come on, Mister Ferrari."

He looked at her warily as she scooted forward a little on the motorcycle and pulled a helmet off the back, handing it to him. He recoiled. "I don't need that."

"I think you do. State law," she said in a firm tone. "Well, my law, anyway."

"I mean, I'm not riding on that hellish hunk of junk! I would really appreciate it if you'd just go call someone for me!" He was thoroughly put out with her hijinks.

"I don't *think* so, you brave, fearless guy. I've got errands to run, but I'll drop you off at the 7-11 and you can call whomever you like and cool off with a Slurpee, too."

"You're generous," he grumbled. The woman was a maniac! She drove rattletraps that flaunted the laws of safety. He eyed her jeans and white T-shirt which clearly emphasized her not-D-cup breasts. Her summery shirt outlined a dainty bra. His mind idly asked what kind of panties a woman who chose unsatisfactory driving equipment wore. "Why do you ride that awful tin can on two wheels?" he demanded crossly, startled by his wayward thoughts. Panties, indeed! Who cared what she had on under those worn-out jeans?

She shrugged. "I couldn't afford a car. I'd rather reinvest my profits in my farm. It's risky enough being a farmer, no sense in running up credit card debt, too. Besides which," she said with her gaze sloping suggestively toward his poor Ferrari, "looks like I got a better bargain than you did. At least mine runs."

"You've got a point, I guess." With trepidation,

he glanced at the motorcycle. "But I need doors to feel safe."

She laughed out loud, her teeth glistening in the already-hot morning sun. "Garrison, the 7-11 is only a few miles away. I promise you you'll be as safe as you were last night when I drove you to the Sonic."

He had no choice. He locked the Ferrari, hoping no one would sideswipe it. Awkwardly, he put the helmet on. She had to help him fasten it, her delicate fingers surprisingly sensual against his chin. Dixie Adams's only purpose in life, he decided, was to torment and make fun of him, irritating him with her smart-alecky humor. He slid onto the seat behind her, telling his racing heart not to be scared. She'd promised him he'd be safe.

It wasn't until he put his hands on the feminine curve of her tiny waist and her perky little bottom slid between his thighs as they pulled up on the road that he realized he wasn't safe at all.

He was in *terrible* danger.

If he didn't know better, he'd almost think he liked it.

NOREEN AWAKENED, becoming slowly aware that her ear was being kissed most seductively. She smiled and moaned, liking the sensation—and waking up with Parker—immensely.

"Good morning." His deep voice was husky in her ear.

She turned her head to look at him. "Good morning to you."

He stared down at her, his lips curved in a half smile she found enormously confident and sexy.

"Look what I found in my bed," he said playfully.

"I was on your lap in a chair when I fell asleep."

"You had to be uncomfortable." His hand slid over the curve of her waist. "I thought you'd sleep better in here."

"I slept fine." It was true. Her dress would have been torture at any other time, but she'd gladly have slept in hay to wake up with Parker. "How about you?"

"Well, the temptation of a beautiful woman in my bed was nearly too much. I thought I might stay awake all night, but," he picked up a strand of her hair which he curled around a finger, "you snore. Right then, I knew I'd be able to sleep."

"Oh, you're mean." Noreen laughed and gave him a slight push on his arm. "I do not snore!" A perplexed frown crossed her face. "I don't, do I?"

"Don't you know?"

"No!" She gave him an exasperated look. "I've never slept with anyone before! So how *would* I know?"

The smile slid from his face, becoming more of a puzzled expression. Noreen hesitated at his sudden seriousness, then realized exactly what she'd said.

"Noreen, you're not saying what I think you just said, are you?" Parker asked carefully.

Her eyelashes slid down for a second before she met his gaze again. "Well, I didn't mean to mention it quite like that."

"Is it true?"

"Yes," she whispered. Her eyes searched his for a reaction, but it was guarded. "Um, maybe I *do* snore. Maybe I just need the right man to...answer this question which has been bothering me."

He didn't say anything.

"I mean," she continued nervously, "maybe I do. Maybe I don't. Maybe it's a life-threatening condition. It happens, you know. But how will I ever find out if..."

"I can't, Noreen," he murmured. "I'd like to, I really would. More than like to. I'd consider myself the luckiest man in the world to make love with you."

She stared up at him. "I hear a *but*."

He shrugged, gently laying the hair he'd twined around his finger back against her breast. "You already turned down my marriage proposal. What's a guy got going for him if he makes love to a woman who won't marry him? Haven't you ever heard that if you give the milk away for free, the cow never gets bought?"

"Oh, stop!" She gave him a thump on the chest, which she noticed immediately was quite hard. Her lips twisted in laughter she wouldn't give him the pleasure of hearing. "You don't make sense about anything."

"I do."

"You don't! You won't make love to me because I won't marry you, which I'm not sure I believe. And you said you weren't sure you'd be able to sleep last night, except that I snored so you could. No one can sleep if someone's snoring in the bed with them! That I *do* know, because when my dad fell asleep when we watched old movies, he sucked in so much wind snoring that it interfered with the reception of the rabbit ears on our TV."

"You caught me," he said obligingly. "If you were a snorer, I couldn't have slept, certainly not as well as I did. I was only teasing."

"So how did you fall asleep, if you didn't find me

unattractive?'' she asked, suddenly feeling her blood heat up as his face neared hers.

"Now *you* caught *me*," he said huskily. "I didn't."

His lips touched hers, and his hand cupped her face. His weight rolled closer to her body, so that she felt his heat. Noreen couldn't help the moan of excitement that escaped her lips. She wound her arms up over his shoulders and pulled him closer. His tongue met hers and she whimpered for more. And still their lips clung together, until she thought she would die from wanting.

He broke away, tenderly looking down into her eyes. "I should get you home. Your relatives are probably worried about you."

She raised her brows. "Are you trying to escape?"

"Yes." He nuzzled her neck and slipped one hand over her breast, rubbing lightly. Noreen gasped from the shocking pleasure that washed over her. "Yes, I am. If you stay much longer, I'll have to give in to the pressure."

"What pressure?" She moved under his hand, hungry for his touch.

"Wanting you. It's the truth," he assured her, running the same hand that had teased her breast up under the skirt of her evening gown, pushing it to her thigh so that he could stroke her legs. "I shouldn't have asked you to marry me last night. If I'd slept with you first, you might have said yes. As it is, it's like reading the last page of the book. I already know what's going to happen."

"Parker, men aren't supposed to think like that!" She couldn't believe how wonderful his hand felt as he caressed her bottom and the inside of her thighs.

"Really? I should just make love to you because I'm a man and you're a woman?"

"Well..." He was confusing her! His hand was doing a magic dance close to her most private place, and she couldn't think of anything but how much she wanted him.

"You don't think it should affect my performance or pleasure because you've already opted out of a serious relationship between us?"

"I don't think that's what I did," she said, defensively reaching to stroke her hand along his chest. One by one, she undid the shirt buttons. "I simply rejected your business offer."

His hand stilled a centimeter below the moist crevice between her legs. "What does that mean?"

She stared into his eyes. "You want a mother for Meg, which I can't blame you for. So you bought the land next to mine as a sweetener, I guess. You said yourself you had an agenda."

"I do. But that agenda hasn't made me ask any other woman to marry me. I could have made my business offer, as you put it, to someone else. But I didn't."

She swept her eyelashes down. "I'm sorry. I shouldn't have put it that way. It was unfair."

He slid her dress back down slowly, an action which filled Noreen with regret. She could feel him withdrawing from her emotionally. It was as if something precious between them had been spoiled. Yet she had a right to know exactly what he'd meant with his marriage proposal. Certainly he'd never mentioned love, and most men didn't just toss off proposals like bad apples from trees. He'd been so cool about it that she hadn't even taken him seriously at first.

"It's all right. As I said, I shouldn't have asked you the way I did. It just came to me last night sometime...maybe when we were leaving the party." He frowned thoughtfully. "I heard someone's watch beep midnight and for some reason I thought, *This woman makes me happy.*" He shrugged at her, taking her fingers from his buttons and held them between his own. "You do. You make me happy."

"I'm glad," she replied.

"You make Meg happy, too." He released her fingers and ran a hand through his hair. "Let's not rush anything right now." He gave her a thoughtful look as he rose from the bed, helping her up. "I'd love to keep you here all day and make love to you about half a dozen times, but that's not what either of us is looking for, even in the short term."

He kissed each of her palms before letting her go, intensifying the disappointed, worried feeling sweeping over her. She felt like he'd closed off a door she couldn't go through anymore. "You're not...upset with me, are you?" She desperately hoped not.

"No. I rushed us last night, and I don't want to rush us today. We knew we had a lot of hurdles to cross, and as you said last night, we don't really know if we're right for each other. No point in muddying the waters."

"No," she said, her lips stiff with unhappiness. Something *had* happened, and although she knew he made sense, she couldn't help feeling like she'd lost him.

Soft knocking on the door shattered the moment.

"Excuse me. I don't know who that could be, unless it's my in-laws and I'm not expecting them yet. Did you order us breakfast in bed?'' he asked.

His tone sounding teasing, but Noreen could tell it was an effort. ''No, I didn't.''

He left the room, and she heard the door open a moment later.

''Daddy!'' she heard Meg shout with delight.

''Hi, sweetheart!''

Noreen smiled. She couldn't wait to see the little girl again. Still, since Parker's in-laws had brought her back, Noreen decided to stay in his bedroom. No point in walking out in last night's clothes—it would embarrass his ex-wife's parents unduly, no doubt. She frowned suddenly. It also wouldn't be right for Meg to see her here, she realized. She and Parker had slept so late—and as he'd said, the in-laws had returned earlier than he'd expected—surely he'd meant to get her home before his daughter returned. Biting her lip, Noreen wondered what to do. There was no way it was a good thing for Meg to see her here—but her shoes were in the other room. She just couldn't exit out a back door and flag down a taxi.

Murmured adult voices filtered back to the bedroom. Though she couldn't hear his words, Parker's tone was unhappy and sharp. Not an indication of the esteem in which he'd appeared to hold his ex-inlaws at all. Noreen waited awkwardly.

''Look, Daddy,'' she heard Meg call, ''I can wear Mommy shoes!''

Heels slap-slapped across the carpet. Noreen frowned—until she realized Meg was playing dress-up in her evening heels! Burning with embarrassment, she closed her eyes, hoping Parker's in-laws could stand the shock of realizing he had an overnight guest.

"Oh, Parker!" she heard a female voice exclaim unhappily. "I...I didn't know you had company. I thought you'd...fallen asleep in your clothes." There was a moment's hesitation which stretched long and strained before the woman rushed on, "I'm sorry. We'll come back later. This afternoon."

"Lavinia—"

"I wanted to talk with you, but we can discuss this later. Come on, sweetie, take the shoes off. We've...caught Daddy at a bad time. We'll come back in a little while."

"It's not necessary to take Meg."

"Meg, honey, come on," the woman insisted, her voice loud and firm. "We'll come back closer to noon."

"She can stay with me. I was just leaving," Parker said.

Noreen crept closer to the door, noting that Parker's statement of an impending departure appeared to silence the woman for a moment. No doubt she was relieved to know whoever was in the bedroom wasn't anticipating a long morning of lovemaking.

"Are you...sure?"

"Positive. What do you want to talk about?"

There was silence for a moment. Noreen squeezed her eyes closed with embarrassment.

"Our marriage," she heard the woman reply.

Chapter Ten

"Here," Parker said a minute later. He handed Noreen her evening shoes as she hovered in the bedroom, her heart having tightened to the size of a pumpkin seed from what she'd overheard. His marriage! His ex-wife sounded like she might want to make amends.

It would put their family back together. Intact, the way Parker wanted. What he wanted for his daughter.

"She's taken a liking to your shoes," he commented. "Haven't you, sweetie?" He kissed Meg's cheek as he put her down. The woman he'd called Lavinia had left, after he'd promised to talk with her later. Noreen had stayed hidden in the bedroom, but Parker had brought Meg right back. She wore a Sunday dress again, as she had the other day, but this time her barrette was straight and her long ringlets combed until they shone—a mother's touch. The child was glad to see Noreen, who accepted her joyous hugs and kisses as if they were gold.

"Aren't you worried about her seeing me here?" she whispered to Parker.

He shrugged. "She saw us together at your house."

"You pwetty, Miss Noreen," Meg said. Her hand

reached out to reverently touch the sparkling beads on the gown.

"Thank you." She hugged the child to her. "Parker, you'd better take me home," she said reluctantly. Their fantasy night was over, and they both had lives to return to. She had a farm; he had a daughter and an ex-wife who had something important to say to him. Lavinia must want him back. The thought hurt worse than Noreen expected it might.

She couldn't blame Lavinia, nor should she stand in the way.

"I'm sure Hattie and crew are plenty worried. Why don't you call them and tell them we're on the way? There's a phone in the kitchen. I'll shower and change while you do that."

"That's a good idea." Breathlessly, Noreen tried to tell herself Parker wasn't anxious to get rid of her. Meg tagged along with her as she went into the small kitchen, which had gourmet copper pots hanging from a ceiling rack and a giant fern splaying its fronds in a corner. She dialed Priscilla's house and told her grandmother she would be there soon.

Ten minutes later, during which time she watched a Sunday-morning cartoon with Meg in her lap, Parker rejoined them. "Ready, ladies? Calls placed to appropriate party, etcetera?"

She smiled, meeting Parker's eyes hesitantly. "Yes."

"Let's go, then." He walked her to the door, and Meg clapped her hands.

"Goody! I want to ride Meanie!"

"Meg, you haven't been invited," Parker remonstrated.

"Yes, she has," Noreen said for Parker's ears only.

The door closed behind them, and he locked it. Noreen couldn't meet his eyes. So much had happened between them, yet they were no more comfortable with each other than they'd been. The thought made her so unhappy.

"She has?" His glance at her was measuring.

"Yes," she assured him. "Anytime you want to bring her to the farm." She and Parker might not ever be able to have an easy relationship, but she knew exactly how to please his child. "Meg has a standing invitation to ride Meanie whenever she likes. That pony will get lazy if someone doesn't."

"Hurray!" Meg shouted.

Noreen smiled at the child, then caught Parker's gaze on her. He wasn't smiling. Suddenly Noreen knew she was trying to act as if nothing had changed.

But everything had changed. And by the look on his face, apparently for the worst where she was concerned.

DIXIE STOPPED at the 7-11, taking off her helmet as soon as she parked the motorcycle. Her gleaming, bronze-highlighted hair fell free, the dancing ponytail brushing past Garrison's nose.

She was far too much free spirit for him.

"Thanks for the ride." He got off and handed the helmet he'd borrowed back to her. "I'll just call a wrecker and have them tow the car to the farm. Do you mind taking me home?"

"Actually, I can't." She shrugged, and her shoulders moved enticingly. "I'm sorry. I really have a lot to get done, and I'm about to head into Dallas." One paprika-colored brow rose disapprovingly. "You know, Garrison, you're kind of a needy guy."

"Needy?"

"Yeah. Not really equipped to fend for yourself."

He didn't like that at all. "I'm doing fine, thanks."

"Garrison, how old are you?"

"Twenty-five. Three years younger than Noreen."

"I see."

"You see what?"

She shook her head. "I'm twenty-five."

"So?"

"Well, I'm very equipped to fend for myself."

"So give yourself a medal," he retorted crossly. "What's that got to do with anything?"

"I don't know. I'm just thinking. Maybe you've got a touch of little-brother syndrome or something. Maybe it's living with four women that's got you..."

He stared at her, his blood starting to boil. "Got me what?" he demanded.

"Got you kind of helpless. Spoiled."

"I am not spoiled *nor* helpless." He shook a finger at her. "You don't know a thing about me. Just start your bike and haul off to wherever you were going, Miss Lippy. I don't know how I ever thought you were...were..." His voice trailed off as he realized what he'd been about to say.

"Were what?"

She cocked her head at him like an inquisitive bird, one he'd like to take home. "Nothing."

He wasn't about to tell her anything about himself. She thought she knew everything, so no doubt there was nothing he could shed any light on for her. Fumbling around in his pockets, he realized he didn't have a dime. He had a quarter to make the phone call, but not the additional dime. Dixie watched him with a bit of disgust, but he told himself to ignore the ornery woman. "Can I borrow a dime?"

She sighed heavily and reached into her jeans, a movement which thrust her not-D-cups out more admirably than he might have imagined. "Here."

"Thanks. For the ride, though not the shrink session." He stalked over to the pay phones, which were outside the 7-11, in a huff. How dare that no-bigger-than-a-minute woman think that he wasn't equipped to deal with life? He could handle anything she could, and better!

To his utmost disbelief, all three of the pay phones were out of order. Dixie sat on her bike, watching him.

It was going to hurt, but he had to do it.

"Dixie," he said, walking back to where she perched on her two-tired transportation, "the pay phones are out. I know you said you were awfully busy today, but if I can talk you into driving me home—please—maybe I can borrow Noreen's truck and help you with some of your errands."

He implored her with his eyes. He really didn't want to stay at this 7-11 until someone else he knew drove up so that he could bum a ride from them.

"All right," she said on a heavy sigh. "Get on, Garrison."

He obeyed before she could change her mind, and put the helmet on without being told a second time.

"You'll run me a little late for my appointment in Dallas, but I'll call and tell the guy I was meeting I'm running behind and it'll be okay," she hollered over her shoulder to the accompaniment of motorcycle roar.

Guy? He hated that thought. What guy would want

such a tiny bumblebee of a woman with beesting-sized—never mind that, he told himself sternly. His destination was Dallas, too.

"I was going into Dallas myself today," he shouted back.

"What part?"

"Downtown."

She turned to look at him. "So was I. How long will your appointment take?"

"Maybe an hour." His heartbeat climbed with hope that his campaign might still be saved. He'd do anything to fit himself to her schedule; he'd be sweet as molasses and not complain any further if she'd take him there. He desperately wanted to leave a personal business card and message for Mr. Crower of Crower Real Estate Investments—and just see if he could land himself a future dinner meeting to discuss selling out of Cinderella Acres. There had to be a way to get around Noreen. Perhaps Mr. Crower could advise him if he were interested enough in his business proposition.

"Mine, too. Maybe it would be faster if we just headed west."

"Fine by me," he said agreeably. "I can call about my car just as easily from Dallas. Of course, I don't want to inconvenience you," he tacked on hurriedly.

"Doesn't matter to me if you're hanging on to the back of my bike, just so long as I get all my chores done today. Hold on!"

She zoomed onto the road and headed up the ramp toward the highway into Dallas. Garrison grinned, tucking his hands around her nicely shaped, jeans-covered hips. *She's just seeing a guy about a chore that she has to get out of the way.* That didn't sound like romance to him, and Garrison was happier about that than the more nefarious reason he was heading into the city.

There probably wasn't a man on earth who would have such a twiggy-legged, opinionated woman, anyway. How dare she assume he was the bottom of the barrel when it came to species selection? He'd show her just how fit he was when he sold his land. Money always brought women running.

But he wouldn't give her the time of day when she did. He would remember that she thought he was needy. Well, he needed a lot of things in life, but he certainly didn't need *her*.

NOREEN WALKED into her house, only to find it unusually quiet and empty. Hattie and Company had left a note on the table. "Turkey sandwiches in the fridge. Hope you had a lovely time, dear. Love, Priscilla, Charlene and Hattie."

"That's so sweet," she murmured. It had been a good time, of sorts, though it hadn't ended on such an enchanted note. "Parker, I'm not really hungry. Would you like a sandwich?"

"No, thanks." He sat in a kitchen chair and pulled Meg up onto his lap. "Your relatives meant to feed you."

It was nearly noon, and neither of them had eaten breakfast as they'd slept late. She hadn't thought about food while she and Parker had lain together in his big bed. Feeling loved had been all she'd craved.

Curiously she pulled the tray from the refrigerator. "I think they either meant for you to join me for lunch, or they're expecting a small army to come marching up the road." Six half sandwiches lay enticingly on a white plate, garnished with lettuce. Beside the plate sat a full pitcher of fresh tea, newly picked mint sitting on top. "You might as well join me. The least I can do is offer you and Meg a snack."

"You talked me into it." He kissed his daughter's cheek. "Are you hungry, sweetie?"

"No." She slid down from his lap and trained her gaze out the window where she could see Meanie grazing. "I had cereal with Mommy this morning, and then a doughnut at church."

Noreen tried not to think about the envy that stung her. She shouldn't be envious. But a haunting worry crept over her that this might be the last time she ever saw Parker—and Meg.

Doing her best to ignore the painful thought, she put a plate with two sandwich halves on it in front of Parker, along with a glass of iced tea.

"Thank you. This looks great."

She smiled dismissively at his attempt to be polite.

"No, really," he said, taking a hearty bite. "You'd be surprised how tiresome it is to always either eat alone, or eat at McDonald's." He whispered the last with a subtle jerk of his head Meg's way. "We eat a lot of French fries and chocolate shakes." Shaking his head, he said, "It's a parent trap. Children have been programmed to drag their parents in there, and they comply in order to see the delight on their child's face when he or she is playing in the toys. And also to be able to consume a double cheeseburger in peace while the child plays. But one day," he said in a low, confidential voice, "my child is going to ask me to take her to a salad bar to eat. I'm prepared to celebrate that day with a stiff, alcoholic drink." He raised his tea glass to Noreen.

She laughed and held hers up, too. They clinked them together, then drank. "You'll have more kids. It could be years before you escape the parent trap."

He froze, then slowly set his glass down. "I hadn't thought of that."

She raised her brows. "You haven't?"

"No. I've been so busy raising this one that I've never considered another." He looked thunderstruck. "In fact, she's four, the perfect age to have a sibling. We'd better get started."

"*We'd* better—" She paused in her astonishment. "We?"

"Meg would love a baby brother or sister." He snapped his fingers. "And of course you'll want children. I should have thought of that when I posed my awkward business proposal last night."

His attitude was mock serious, but she sensed his underlying question. She sipped her drink, stalling for time. "I might want children one day."

"You should. Genes like yours should be propagated. There's some farm talk for you." He nodded seriously, but gave her a tiny, teasing pinch on the arm. "I won't be one of those husbands who isn't interested in what my wife does for a living. And I'll rub your feet at night when you come in from the fields. I'm a champion foot massager," he bragged.

"He rubs my back at night when I go to sleep," Meg confirmed.

Noreen started. The child had been so still, so mesmerized by Meanie grazing in the paddock that she hadn't realized she was listening. She felt guilty even joking around about marrying Parker when Meg's mother had arrived in town on an apparent mission. Briskly, she stood, taking her plate to the sink.

Meg turned her head eagerly. "Can I ride now, Miss Noreen? Please?"

"What good manners you have, Meg." Not only had she said please, but waited patiently until the adults were through with lunch to ask. Noreen was finished, her appetite completely gone. Parker continued eating with gusto. But her heart was too worried to take any pleasure in the meal. "Tell you what, Meg. Keep your daddy company while he finishes eating. Let me shower and change," she said, stroking Meg's silky hair. "Then you can help me saddle Meanie up."

"Okay." Meg appeared as content as any four-year-old could be with yet another delay.

Noreen smiled as Meg crawled into her daddy's lap and reached for his tea glass. But he wasn't paying any attention to that. His eyes were on Noreen, his lips turned up in a half smile. "I may try my hand at saddling Meanie up, just to see if I can figure it out myself. I've ridden once or twice."

"I'm sure you can figure it out, so help yourself. I'll be down shortly." She returned his smile, but noticed with an appreciative shiver that his gaze slipped down the curved length of her evening gown.

"We'll head to the barn now." His lingering gaze roamed back to meet hers.

Was he uncomfortable to stay in the house while she showered? "Don't rush your lunch. Stay as long as you like."

"I'm all done." He hurriedly drank the last of his tea.

"I didn't mean to rush you out."

"Are you kidding? By now, I'm usually getting

dragged into a ball pit at McDonald's. That was the most leisurely lunch I've had in a while.''

"Don't you have slow-paced business lunches? The proverbial two-martini lunch?" He was so successful at what he did she couldn't imagine him not spending a lot of time currying that business.

He shrugged. "What's relaxing about doing business over lunch? It's a guaranteed recipe for indigestion." Swinging Meg up into his arms, which elicited a happy squeal from his child, he said, "No. I'd rather eat disgusting, cold French fries and glutinous double-cheeseburgers with my baby any day."

Father and daughter stared at each other for a second, nose-to-nose. "Oh, Daddy, you silly," Meg admonished. "What's glutinous?"

He blew a raspberry into the side of her neck. "A word you'll probably hear again one day when you start wearing makeup, little lady. So remember it. Glutinous."

She giggled, not understanding, but adoring her father's attention. Noreen held the door open so he could walk out with his child. The thought hit her as they walked past that for once in her life she was more worried about her heart than her crops. Her pumpkins were doing fine; they lay soaking up the hot Texas sun.

The pleasure that sight would normally bring her shriveled into a tight knot inside her soul. Despite Parker's banter about them having children together, he could have more children with Lavinia—if that was what he wanted. She could hardly ask him what place in his life his ex-wife held.

Just now he sounded less like he was discussing a business proposal than a marriage proposal. Could he mean it? Her hopeful heart soared. He said he'd be interested in her work, not put off by the long hours she spent in the fields. He had mentioned marriage twice in two days. That was a good sign, wasn't it? And he didn't seem eager to get back to Dallas to talk with his wayward ex. Maybe all of this boded well.

Of course, Noreen thought as she watched Parker and Meg walk toward the barn, he'd loved Lavinia. Had admitted it had taken a long time to get over marrying the wrong woman, though he was grateful for Meg. He and Noreen weren't in love with each other. Which brought her back to the business arrangement theory.

They'd have dinner together some nights, most likely without two martinis, since Meg would hopefully be with them. It would consist of nutritious food and an appealing dessert. Iced tea, of course, maybe milk for Meg. All the major components of the food pyramid, served with a contented smile, as the three of them sat in their preassigned seats at the table. Strictly bread and business.

But will I also give him indigestion?

Chapter Eleven

Noreen couldn't stand it any longer. Meg had run out the door to stand on the split rails of the paddock, so now was as good a time as any to broach the question that was killing her. She didn't think she'd be able to breathe properly until she knew.

"Parker." Her voice softly stayed his exit from the house.

"Yes?" He raised his brows questioningly as he stared down into her eyes.

"It's probably none of my business, but...I got the feeling you were a bit surprised to see— Well, that is, I was surprised, too, but I couldn't help overhearing her say..." She trailed off, realizing she wasn't winning any awards for clarity. "Parker," she said, her voice strained, "doesn't your ex-wife change things?"

He was silent for a long moment before shaking his head. "No. She doesn't change a thing. Any other questions?"

"Well—" Yes! She had a million! But he didn't seem too eager to talk about his ex-wife. Still, her heart told her to be brave and ask what she wanted to, or else suffer the uncertainty of her curiosity.

"You said you wanted a whole family for Meg. I suppose your ex-wife returning might solve that."

He shook his head. "Not to paint her as a villain, but with Lavinia, it does not."

"I have the oddest feeling of being in the way," she confessed.

"I'm sorry you feel that way. You don't know me very well if you think I'd still be here if there was the remotest chance I'd get back together with Lavinia. But as we discovered last night, we have to spend more time getting to know each other. That's why I'm here."

Her spirits lifted. "I hoped you'd say that."

"Did you?"

"Yes! Of course, I'd understand if you—"

"Noreen. Don't second-guess me. Don't try to fix my love life. I'm not Garrison, and I don't need you taking care of me. Lavinia might want to come back but she'd leave again. Yes, us getting back together would give Meg a whole family, but when Lavinia left us again, Meg would also suffer a broken heart. She was too young to remember her mother leaving the first time, and assumes that it's normal for Lavinia to be gone. Sort of like a relative who lives out of state." He sighed heavily. "I hope that doesn't sound callous. But try to see my side. Lavinia left me. She went to find herself, and in the meantime found a hippie artist who indulged her creative side. Yes, I could take her back at the expense of my pride, something I'd do for Meg. But I'm not exactly a skip-the-shaving, grow-my-hair-to-my-waist kind of guy. She may be laboring under some kind of false illusion that she needs to come home, but knowing Lavinia, I'd say it's more likely a financial situation that has brought her back than true love for either Meg or myself. And I suspect her sudden mention of our marriage was more for the benefit of the overnight guest she realized I had than for me."

"Oh, dear." Noreen wanted to cry for him and his beautiful child. "I'm sorry, Parker. And I didn't mean to pry."

He put his hands lightly on her shoulders, holding her so that he could look into her eyes. "I'm glad you asked, Noreen. Believe me, I'd rather one of my stock portfolios take a nosedive into the deep than discuss my ex-wife. But it's a beautiful Sunday afternoon, I've got a little girl who's anxious for her pony ride and a lovely lady I'm itching to spend the rest of the day getting to know better." He leaned down and kissed her lightly on the lips. "I'm afraid I'm falling for you pretty hard, Noreen. I really wasn't looking to fall in love again, but it does appear I don't have a whole lot of control where you're concerned."

She loved hearing that. Her heart had been so frightened by the thought of falling for Parker when he wasn't available! "All right. I'll go shower and be right back."

"You're not the only one with reservations, Noreen," he said softly. "My daughter invited herself for a pony ride, which has made it a very convenient excuse for me to hang around you today. I guess you'd tell me if you wanted us to leave."

"I would, but I don't." Especially now that he'd soothed her worries about Lavinia.

"Okay. Then I'm off to figure out the difference between a girth and a halter. Poor pony."

She smiled as he went out, closing the screen behind him. She was living a dream again, one with a happy ending on the horizon. Absolutely nothing could ruin her happiness now.

GARRISON FINISHED up at Crower Real Estate, elated with his success. He nearly ran down the stairs to meet Dixie, who sat on her nonconformist conveyance waiting for him.

"All done?" she called.

"Yes!" He jumped on her bike and jammed his helmet on his head. "You?"

"Got it taken care of." She turned to look at him. "Garrison, you went to see Crower, didn't you?"

His fingers tightened on the helmet strap. "How did you guess?"

"I can read a sign." She jerked her head toward the building lobby.

"You don't have any business checking up on me," he said defensively.

"I wasn't, really. I had some time to kill, so I wandered inside."

He didn't like the disappointed tone of her voice. "So I went to see Crower. What of it?"

"Well, it's not too hard to put two and two together. I shouldn't have told you that Crower got outbid on the land behind yours. You're going to try to get Noreen to sell, aren't you?"

"Not that it's any of your affair," he ground out, "but I happen to own half that farm. Well, almost half." He would control more than fifty percent once he got the aunts to side with him. They didn't want to end up in retirement homes, but that's just where they'd go if Noreen's crops failed another year. There was no more money in savings, not the amount she'd need to cover her losses. Of course, the pumpkin crop was doing quite well, he'd noticed, but one good hail-storm or blight would take care of that. Mother Nature usually managed to keep Noreen just at the poverty level. He didn't understand why she chose to keep working the dry, dusty soil when she could sell the farm and live well. ''Someone's got to be the business head in this family. Noreen sure doesn't have any fiscal sense. If the land behind us sold for a fortune, why should we continue to live like paupers?''

Dixie's eyes regarded him steadily. She turned away in silence, starting the engine of the motorcycle. He didn't care if she didn't like his plans. It was none of her concern!

Suddenly the bike roared away from the curb so fast he had to clamp his hands around her to keep from landing on his rear in the street. Bossy, nosy woman! He didn't care if she gave him the silent treatment.

Well, he did care a little, but he wasn't going to bother to justify himself. Dixie could ignore him all she pleased.

He did wish she hadn't found out where he'd gone, though. Her condescending disapproval stung more than he thought it would.

Thirty minutes later he realized the bike wasn't headed home. He frowned, tired of riding so far on such an uncomfortable vehicle. Dixie hadn't mentioned that she was taking him on any of the other errands she had to do today.

''Where are we going?'' he called over her shoulder.

She didn't reply. Garrison cocked his brows with displeasure. His Ferrari didn't have this wind problem. People could hear each other talk. "I said, where are we going?"

Almost instantly she turned off the highway, heading down a side road. Two minutes later they bumped onto an open dirt path which led to rows and rows of green corn stalks. She parked the motorcycle between two rows and killed the engine, pulling her helmet from her head in one smooth movement. He was almost so mesmerized by her actions that he nearly forgot to inject displeasure into his features. "What are you doing?"

"I have to start my farm chores. You can help me."

He was astonished. Jerking his helmet from his head, he gave her his most high-and-mighty glare. "I will not."

"Then walk home." She turned, leaving him sitting astride the bike. "Helping me is the least you can do since I hauled your sorry butt into town." Striding away, she called, "I shouldn't have done it. I should have left you to rot by the side of the road with your stupid, overpriced, pickup-mobile."

"Hey!" He didn't like that at all. He didn't have to pick up women; they usually fell into his arms. "You can't hold me hostage, Dixie, just because you don't like my plans."

"I sure as heck can." She swiveled on a heel to face him from about a hundred feet away, standoff style. "I may have hurt Noreen by aiding you, but that was the least of my intentions. I may have hurt her sweet family because of you, and I really don't like the sensation of nursing an asp to my bosom."

That caught Garrison's full attention. He didn't like her reference to him as an asp, but his gaze instantly went to her not-D-cups. Funny how he was attracted to this tiny woman in spite of himself. He didn't want to be, that was for certain!

"I mean, you're such a rodent you didn't even bother to offer to pay for my gas. Or split it with me." She stared at him angrily. "I'm not taking you one more inch, you traitor. And I've got a good mind to call your sister and warn her about what you're up to. They say information is power, and I'll just bet Noreen needs all the power she can muster to deal with you."

She disappeared into a row of plants, leaving Garrison to stare after her in astonishment. What a mouth that itty-bitty woman had on her!

"Uh, Dix," he called. Shoot, he sure hoped there were no rattlers around. He'd always heard snakes and corn crops went together. His Italian snakeskin loafers weren't made for running if a reptile decided to slither up and check out its species. "Dix, I'm sorry I made you mad. I should have offered to pay for your gas. You've been really great. How can I get you to take me home?"

There was silence for a moment before she answered. "I think manual labor is the only way I'll feel repaid, Garrison."

"I will *not* work in your fields like a common—" He bit that off, realizing he was about to dig himself in further. Farming was her livelihood, after all.

"You will *not* go home, then. Unless you walk."

He couldn't stand being manipulated by someone he couldn't see. It was impossible to work his charm on Dixie when she wouldn't look at him. Folding his arms across his chest, he decided he'd sit on the motorcycle until she wore out her antagonism. Sooner or later she'd have to come back and get her bike so that she could go home.

Then he'd give *her* a choice: either she took him home to his place or hers. He couldn't wait to see the look on Miss Lippy's face when she received an ultimatum of her own.

Two hours later he was hot from the sun and boiling mad from his temper. When that snippy woman came back for him, he was going to tell her just what he thought of her. He was hungry and thirsty, and his pride was completely bent out of shape. Dixie Adams was a whole passel of trouble in a tiny package.

Her face suddenly peeped around a corn row, startling him half to death.

"Aarrgh!" He leaped off the motorcycle. "What in the heck do you think you're doing? You get over here right now and take me home!"

She walked over, assessing his clothes, which were stuck to him with sweat. "What the heck have *you* been doing?"

"Waiting on you to quit being such a wacko! Did it ever once occur to you that I could have been bitten by a snake?"

"No."

Her bright eyes fixed on him quite seriously, but he saw the smile she was trying to hide. "Now look here, I know you probably think it was very funny to shanghai me and leave me in the middle of nowhere, but it wasn't. Nobody's laughing, Dixie Adams!"

She giggled. "You're right. Nobody's laughing."

"You take me home!"

"I can't. You're still a rude little boy, and I don't take kindly to the way you talk to me. Nobody's keeping you, Garrison. You can walk home. You can walk up to the highway and hitch a ride. So quit crying just because you can't have everything your way.''

"I tell you, Dixie—'' He bit off the threat he wanted to utter, because she'd only laugh at him harder. "I wouldn't walk miles through fields and ruin my shoes. That would be dumb. Furthermore, I'm going to tell your grandfather how irresponsible you are.''

Now she did burst out laughing, making his ears ring. She held her stomach, gasping in great gulps of air, she laughed so hard. He crossed his arms stubbornly over his chest. The woman was missing a few cogs in her clock, obviously.

"Oh, Garrison,'' she wheezed helplessly, tears of mirth streaming from her eyes, "you are so…so dignified!''

He didn't know what to make of that. She was making fun of him, he was sure, but her point escaped him. Of course he was dignified. She was not. That was one of the many things that separated them. In better circles, it was known as class. She had none, while he was steeped in it. "If you're through with your attack of hysteria, can we go?''

She wiped her eyes. That's when he noticed she had on different clothes than she'd worn on the trip into Dallas. Plus, she looked cool and inviting, not sweat-melted like him. "Where have you been?'' he demanded.

"Inside.'' The look she gave him was totally innocent.

"Inside where?''

"My house." She pointed through the cornfields. "It's just over there."

He swiveled to look, but couldn't see anything. "You left me out here to die of heatstroke while you...you were enjoying air-conditioning?"

"Mmm-hmm. And a shower and a nap." She shrugged at him, quite the sinless Eve. "You could have come in anytime you liked. I just figured you were being your usual stubborn self."

"Usual— Dixie Adams, no one is more stubborn than you!" He pointed at her, completely put out. "I don't appreciate your behavior, nor do I find it amusing!"

"I wasn't trying to be particularly humorous." But she still had laughter in her big eyes.

Arguing was going to get him nowhere. She was immune to threats and manipulation. He knew it was time to try his considerable charm on her. "Can I talk you into taking me inside to cool off? Please? I'm roasting."

"Sure. Come on."

His jaw dropped. He couldn't believe how easy that had been. Docilely he followed her the short distance through the cornfield, noticing how nicely she had everything rowed. It was actually the cleanest, most organized field he'd ever seen. No bugs. No straggly weeds.

A tiny, white-painted house suddenly appeared, like a vision rising up out of the green. Lace curtains hung country-style at every window, and a big black-and-white collie lay on the porch in between two rockers.

It wasn't a bachelor pad, that was for certain. "Nice place, Dix," he said grudgingly. Of course, he would never live in such a dollhouse, and there would never be a hound on his porch, but he could see how the setup suited her.

"Thanks," she said proudly. "It isn't big, but it's all I need." Walking up onto the porch, she patted the dog's head, who raised itself to eye him cautiously. "This is Rascal."

"Hi, Rascal." He wanted Rascal to go away before he decided to come over for a pat, which would leave fur all over his nice trousers. Well, they'd been nice and dry-cleaned before Dixie left him to die in her outdoor, earthen sauna.

Rascal eyed him stoically and didn't come any closer.

"Hmm, that's strange. He's usually so friendly." Dixie shrugged and opened the door. "Make yourself at home for a little while."

The air-conditioning was heaven. Garrison wanted to pull off his clothes and lie under a vent to get the full effect of sheer ecstasy.

"You better eat something so you'll be able to get a whole afternoon in," she instructed from the kitchen.

"Dixie, I hate to break this to you, but I'm not doing any work for you." Best they get that fact straight right away.

"Okay. I'm not taking you home, then," she called pleasantly.

"I'll phone my sister to come get me." He meandered into the kitchen, where she was making up two bacon, lettuce and tomato sandwiches.

"Fine. If your conscience can stand it, the phone's in the hall."

"What do you mean, if my conscience can stand

it?'' He came to stand beside her to look at the food she was preparing. Suddenly he realized how good she smelled, fresh and clean and just plain Dixie. Her hair lay smoothed back from her face in its typical shiny ponytail, which showed off her beautiful eyes and wonderful complexion. *She really is pretty,* he thought irrationally. *For a country girl,* he reminded himself. No sense getting carried away when she wasn't his type at all.

"If your conscience can stand the fact that you were just in Dallas looking for a buyer for your sister's land, who has no idea she's about to be coerced into selling something." Dixie paused as she looked up into his eyes. "Garrison, wouldn't that bother you? A little?"

"I..." He'd never thought of it that way. The only thing he'd had on his mind was keeping his Ferrari from creditors. He'd sunk practically every penny he owned into buying that dream machine, and maneuvering to keep it pretty much consumed his thoughts. Suddenly he realized Dixie was right. "Maybe I should call a cab."

"Can you pay for one, or does Noreen get stuck with the tab?"

He couldn't afford a twenty-dollar taxi ride, but he resented her commonsense tone. Obviously, by Dixie's standards, he couldn't shaft Noreen on the one hand and make her pay for his ride home on the other. Sighing, he said, "I suppose you'll have some suggestion that suits your high-minded conscience."

She went back to laying juicy red tomato slices on the bread. "You could always get a job, Garrison. Pay for your own ticket in life."

He brushed his trousers off. "I guess." Dixie probably wouldn't be impressed by the fact that he hadn't worked a day in his life. He'd gone to a community college on his inheritance money, where he'd made dismal grades because he'd been too busy with a party curriculum. He'd sweet-talked a few girls of good social standing into inviting him home, thereby earning a reputation as a sought-after kind of guy. And he'd buddied up with other guys from good, moneyed backgrounds, so he always had opportunities to be seen in the right circles. Nobody had ever realized he was pretty much a professional sponge— until Dixie. He frowned at her, but she didn't look at him. "Get a job doing what?"

"I don't know." She lifted her shoulders in a deliberate shrug. "Today you can help me in the fields to pay me back for the gas you bummed chasing down a bad idea. Then tomorrow you could go talk to Grandpa. He's hiring."

"At his taxi company?" Garrison was incredulous. "You've got to be kidding!"

"Why?" She looked up at him, totally serious. "Your car's out of commission. You'll need wheels. No way you'll be able to afford to get it repaired. So you need a job to be able to pay the bill for whatever's wrong with it. And," she said, staring into his eyes, "it's a first baby step on the road to respectability."

He stared at her, struck dumb by the very concept.

Chapter Twelve

Noreen heard the phone ringing when she walked back inside with Meg and Parker. "Put Meg in the bed you slept in before, Parker," she called, hurrying to catch the call. The child was exhausted after spending a sunny Sunday afternoon riding Meanie. "Hello?"

"May I speak to Garrison Cartwright?"

"He's not in right now." The Ferrari wasn't parked out front, so he hadn't returned while she was in the paddock. "I'll be happy to take a message."

"This is Jefferson Crower, of Crower Real Estate Investments. Garrison left some information at my office about a property in Rockwall he was interested in selling."

Noreen's heart felt like it stopped. "Property in Rockwall?"

"Yes. Can I leave you my number so he can return my call?"

"Certainly," she responded automatically, though her lips were numb. Her insides felt icy and pained. What was Garrison up to? He didn't own any land...except part of Cinderella Acres.

She wrote the information down. "I'll give him the message."

"Thank you." The line cut off.

Parker came down the stairs, halting at her worried expression. "What is it?"

"I'm not sure." She shook her head, dazed. "Someone just called from Crower Real Estate about buying some property. Apparently, Garrison contacted him."

"I know Jefferson Crower. He's not the world's nicest human being." Parker walked over to glance at the note. "Does Garrison have any property you're not aware of?"

She wanted to laugh, but it was a reaction to her nervous emotions. "Garrison spends every penny of his monthly allotted inheritance on fast cars and loose women." Instantly she was ashamed by what she'd said and risked a nervous glance at Parker. What must he think of her uncalled-for bitterness? After all, Garrison had lost his mother *and* stepfather—he'd suffered so much. She'd always tried to believe that if he'd had the parental support that every child needed he might have turned out better. He wasn't a bad seed, as the aunts occasionally muttered to each other when they thought Noreen wasn't listening. She'd waited patiently, always hoping that time would help him make something of himself. But the truth was, she was angry about the intrusion of Mr. Jefferson Crower in her life. If Garrison thought he was going to figure out a way to sell part of her land to finance that Ferrari, he was sadly mistaken. For Cinderella Acres, she was prepared to fight. "All he has is what you're standing on, *my* farm."

Parker heard the possessive pronoun—and the

change in Noreen's attitude. "I don't want to poke my nose in where it doesn't belong, but before you let this trouble you, maybe you ought to wait to get Garrison's story."

"As if he'd tell me the truth!" Noreen crossed her arms, putting up a defensive shield. "He's…never been a very honest person."

Parker hated to see her getting upset. "Noreen, he can't sell anything you don't agree to. Right?"

"You don't understand." She paced to the other side of the foyer and back again. "Garrison is… slippery."

"Noreen," Parker said uncertainly, "if you don't trust him, why do you let him stay here, especially since he doesn't contribute anything?"

"It's his home, too," she said with a frown, as if Parker weren't capable of understanding the situation. "Anyway, surely he wouldn't want to sell part of his home."

"No. Listen, I've known Jefferson Crower a long time. He could be calling out here just to test the waters. No doubt he's hungry since I got the land he wanted."

"How do you know that?" Noreen's gaze shot to his.

"The farmer's wife told me. Mrs. Martin also told me that Jefferson wasn't too happy that she sold me her land." Parker shrugged. "We're rivals from way back."

"Well, I'm not going to like being an instrument of revenge," Noreen said hotly. "Although how Garrison could have found out that Jefferson Crower was bidding on Mrs. Martin's property, I don't know."

"Listen, Noreen." He reached out to catch her

hand in his. "Let's go sit down and relax awhile. You don't have anything to worry about. If it takes your signature to sell even a square inch of Cinderella Acres, then I'll make sure no pen ever makes its way into your hand. Remember the king in Sleeping Beauty who ordered all the spinning wheels burned so that his daughter wouldn't prick her finger on a spindle?" He was happy to see the smile he'd coaxed on Noreen's face. "Hey, I read my daughter all the good fairy tales, don't worry."

"As a farmer, I always thought burning the spinning wheels was bad economy," she replied with a lifted brow. "I couldn't help thinking that an entire industry had been wiped out, from cotton growers to pickers to spinners to weavers, all because of a spindle. As a child, I thought it would have been much simpler to snap the spindles off and burn them instead, and instruct the king's wise men to come up with a replacement part. Don't you think so?" she asked him earnestly. "I mean, every king has wise men in his court, or a wizard. Not that you're not doing a good job raising Meg. I don't mean to imply that," she said hastily.

"Well, I'd have to review the kings in history to see if they'd had people around them who were wise, if we're going to say all kings have wise men," he said, drawing her toward him with a purposeful hand. "And I know you weren't criticizing my fathering skills, just shedding new light on the interpretation of fairy tales in the developing minds of young ladies."

She allowed him to pull her close. "Okay, most kings had to have had wise men, then. Just *most*. Otherwise, what's the purpose of having a court?" She laid her forehead against his chin. "I bet Meg loves having her daddy read to her."

"You're avoiding my point about this whole fairy-tale thing." When he pulled her up against him, he moved his hands up to gently cradle her face. "I'm telling you that I'd burn all the pens in Rockwall before I'd let you sign something you didn't want to. And yes, Meg puts two books in her bed every night for me to read to her."

"Let me be the first to praise her very literate father." She stared into his eyes. "All I'm telling you is that there has to be a better way than burning pens, Daddy Charming," she whispered. "Think of the impact on the industry. Writers couldn't write, people couldn't sign checks, doctors couldn't prescribe—"

"Okay," he said on a laugh. "I'm trying to be romantic, Miss Practical."

"I know." She leaned up to kiss him once, ever so lightly, on the lips. "Don't think your chivalry hasn't gone unappreciated."

"No?"

"Absolutely not."

This time he kissed her, a little more lingeringly than she'd kissed him. Parker closed his eyes, enjoying the smooth, warm ribbon of Noreen's mouth under his.

"Of course, my grandmother and aunts could sign their ownership over to Garrison. That would be the only way he could get around me," she murmured.

He paused and opened his eyes, but didn't quite remove his lips from hers. "I got the feeling they were firmly aligned with you."

"I think so."

"Why don't you just buy Garrison out, if money

is all he wants? Then he could hotfoot it off in his Ferrari to some nudist colony somewhere and you wouldn't have to bother with him anymore.'' He scooped Noreen up and carried her into the parlor, where he sat down on a love seat with her in his lap.

''I don't have any money. And now that you've bought Mrs. Martin's land at an escalated price,'' she said with a small frown, ''Garrison will want that much more.''

''I've got it.'' He slid his hands under her white crop top and circled her waist. ''I'll buy Garrison's share.''

''You can't. That would make us business partners, and I'd rather not be business partners with someone who's proposed to me.''

He laughed. ''Look, I'm trying to help you. I thought buying Mrs. Martin's farm would be a nice incentive to get you to marry me, but since that didn't work, I could buy out Garrison.''

''But it's all still business then, Parker, and I don't want to be part of a business deal.'' Her expression became troubled. ''I'd feel like you were buying a mother for Meg if you married me. And if you became my partner, I'd only feel like you pitied me.''

''Where did that come from?'' He frowned at her. ''I don't pity you at all. That's an emotion I reserve for Garrison, who can't even fix himself a meal.''

''I hate to rehash another fairy tale, but Cinderella didn't have a dime and she was just lucky that the prince married her. But I wonder if he felt sorry for her. I mean, you have to know that their relationship was off-kilter from the start. He rescued her, so she was always in his debt.''

''Noreen Cartwright!'' Parker couldn't help his

astonishment. "Are you saying love at first sight is impossible?" That didn't bode well for *him*. He'd already told her he'd fallen for her the first time he'd laid eyes on her.

"I'm saying I don't want to feel indebted to anyone," she told him, her hands going under her shirt to remove his from where they rested against her waist.

He felt her withdraw from him, and something more. He had the strangest sensation that she had drawn a line in the sand he wasn't to step over. "Maybe we should forget about fairy-tale characters, then, and just concentrate on us." Refusing to let go of her fingers, he put both their hands together on top of her waist. "Where do you see our relationship going? I have to ask, since you've already decided I'm some kind of rescuer you have to avoid."

She lowered her eyelashes for a moment, then met his gaze uncomfortably. "I don't know where I see us going. There's never been much time in my life for anything but my farm."

He digested that. "Casual dating is all it's going to be."

"At least for right now." She struggled to sit up and wiggle out of his lap, and he let her. "You know, Parker, I have to say I'm not quite comfortable with you. Since you've come into my life, I've had to say the word *sell* an awful lot, as in, I'm not going to sell my land. It makes me nervous."

That caused his temper to flare. "I am not the snake-in-the-grass you're trying to portray me as. Garrison is the one who asked me to buy his land. Garrison is the one who obviously has gone hunting another prospective buyer."

She thought about that for a moment. "But it never happened before."

"So?"

"I think I'll never really know, Parker. I said before that dating a successful real estate developer was probably going to be difficult for me."

"You think I have underhanded motives." He leaned back against the sofa and stretched his legs out in a purposefully casual pose. "Let's see—I bought Widow Martin's land, and now I'm romancing you and offering to buy Garrison's share to give you peace of mind, but my true incentive is the water theme park with high-rise hotels I want to build right next to where you grow pumpkins." He turned to look at her. "Oh, wait, there's more. After I trick you into marrying me—so that Meg can have a mother—I'll pour concrete over your pumpkin patch and grow a gambling casino for the adults' nighttime diversion after a day with the kiddies." He got to his feet.

She caught his hand, staying him. "Please don't be mad. I don't know what I think. I'm just feeling under siege."

He removed his hand. "Noreen, I don't think I can expect much more from a woman who views fairy tales with such a cynical eye, to be honest. It's the same way you view me. And it means that, no matter how hard I try, my best efforts at pleasing you will be looked on with suspicion."

She stood, too. "I have to be careful, Parker."

"Careful, yes. But I've given you no reason to believe that I'd hurt you, Noreen." He headed up the stairs.

"Wait, Parker," she softly called.

"What?" He barely turned to look at her. He couldn't. It hurt too much.

"Don't go. Especially not mad."

"I think it's for the best." His feelings were hurt, and knowing that this woman would probably never feel the same way about him that he felt about her was painful.

"If I'm giving you the benefit of the doubt about your wife showing up," she said, her tone somewhat snappish, "I think it's safe to say that you can cut me a little slack, too. We've both got some baggage, and we'll either deal with it or not."

She had a point, he admitted to himself. Maybe she had a few reasons to be cautious. "I'll admit you handled Lavinia's unexpected appearance better than I would have imagined," he allowed, quite generously, he thought.

"A heck of a lot better than you would have handled a man showing up on my porch wanting to talk to me about our previous relationship," she shot back.

He bit the inside of his cheek. "I think it's safe to say I would find that disagreeable."

She moved up the stairs, one by one. "Have a jealous streak, do you?"

"Not...heretofore. And I prefer to think of it as a new, cautious side to my nature. Caution is a trait I learned from a farm girl I met recently."

She laughed at him as she gained the same step he stood on. Staring into his eyes, she said, "Then you should learn something else from her."

"What's that?"

"To give people the benefit of the doubt."

"Would she give it to me?"

"She has," Noreen whispered against his chin. Her

whole body relaxed into his, and Parker put his arms around her with a sense of glad relief. "But she has to give it to her stepbrother, too."

"Darn it," he murmured against her hair. "In spite of the fact that he's obviously working against you?"

"That's the point of offering the benefit of the doubt. As you said, Crower might have contacted him. Maybe you should sell Mr. Crower Widow Martin's land."

He paused in the act of running one hand down the back of Noreen's jeans. "Why?"

"You said you were rivals and that it probably made him mad that you outbid him." She stared up into his eyes. "Right?"

"Most likely. We've gone neck and neck on several deals."

"So maybe you've brought this acrimonious relationship of yours with you, right to my doorstep."

He leaned his head back, considering. "Possibly. But I can't sell him something I bought intending to give to you."

"If that's true, why not?" She eased his chin down so he'd have to look at her.

"I…just can't. That's all I can say on that subject, Noreen." He ran his lips along her forehead to kiss her temple, making Noreen sigh with longing. "You'll have to trust me on this one," he told her. "And my acquisition isn't going to change anything if Garrison is trying to sell his part of Cinderella Acres, anyway."

"No," Noreen said huskily, "but it might change something for me. Do you remember telling me you didn't need me to fix your personal life for you? That you were a big boy?"

He tweaked her on the behind for that one. "Yes."

"Well, I don't need you fixing my financial life for me. I'm a big girl. There's something more important than relying on someone else, at least where I'm concerned."

She wasn't looking to be rescued. She wanted the gift of trust, which he'd accidentally put in question with his purchase, no matter how much he'd meant to please her. "I wouldn't call you a big girl," he said huskily. "I would say you're the most beautiful woman I ever met, and I'd rather do a whole lot of other things with you besides hurt you." He kissed behind her ear and nipped suggestively at the lobe. "Wouldn't you?"

She gently tugged him up the stairs toward her bedroom. "Yes. We could take a nap. I need one, like Meg."

"I could use one myself," he agreed. "I had this beautiful woman in my bed last night who snored."

"Not that fairy tale again," she said, laughing. "I'll never believe that I snored."

He drew her close to him, where he sneaked a hand under her shirt to trace her breast. "No. It wasn't the truth."

"I know it wasn't." She nipped along his collarbone, and slowly pulled his shirt from his pants. "But you see how important trust is."

He sighed deeply. "I've earned money faster than your trust."

"I never said dating me was going to be easy." Pulling him to her bed, Noreen sank onto the bedspread. "In fact, I believe I warned you."

"It'll be worth the effort, though." He put one knee between her legs, gently easing her back onto the bed as he looked down into her eyes. "You're worth my best efforts."

"Do you mean that?" She gazed up into his eyes, hardly able to allow herself to believe that Parker might be as crazy for her as she was beginning to feel for him. Everything was almost too perfect—but she had an idea she was going to love being in love.

"Yeah. The riskiest investments sometimes pay off the biggest." He lay down beside her and ran a palm along her cheek. "I'll always be honest with you, Noreen. I promise." He kissed along the path his hand had gone, stopping at her ear to whisper, "You drooled."

"I did not!" She pushed him away playfully. "Why are you so intent on torturing me about my sleep habits?"

"I think," he whispered against her hair as he held her close, "that teasing you is the only way I can keep from giving in to what I really want to do with you."

"Oh." She closed her eyes. It was so wonderful to know that he wanted her as much as she wanted him. She admired him for being a man who wouldn't date her lightly—but by nature, she was much too level-headed to allow herself to impetuously fall head-over-heels in love, even if she was already halfway there. It was so scary! And exciting…

She sighed, snuggling up against him. "I understand. I didn't want to tell you this, because I've heard the male ego is a ferocious thing, but…you tell bad knock-knock jokes in your sleep."

"I don't think so." He wrapped his arms around her tightly, reaching for a strand of hair that he gave a mock tug. "Ask Meg. I can never remember any joke after I've heard it."

"But it's true," she insisted without opening her eyes. She just allowed herself to enjoy being this close to Parker's warmth. "Only you never get to the punchline," she murmured, on the edge of drifting to sleep. "You say knock-knock, then who's there? Then you repeat who's there, and that's all. It went on long enough I began to wonder if you might really be a robot." She shrugged. "But then I just figured Meg had been trying to teach you jokes and you hadn't quite gotten the hang of it."

"I've got the hang of you," he growled in her ear, "and you teasing me isn't working. I still want you."

"Oh. Well, then you try it. Knock-knock."

"Who's there?" he muttered, closing his eyes as he rested his chin on top of her head.

She didn't say anything.

"Who's there?" he repeated.

"See? It's so weird," she murmured. "You do it several times a night."

He chuckled. "You she-devil."

"Now go to sleep." Noreen drew in a deep, comfortable breath and told herself to do the same. Sleep wasn't exactly what she wanted from Parker, either, but right now, napping was safe. The alternative would just get them in deeper.

"I'M ROASTING!" Garrison complained. "Surely I've worked off what little gas that hopped-up bike used." He'd been pulling stray weeds from a back field Dixie hadn't finished tending, and then checking stalks and leaves for bugs. That little lady worked *hard*. Not once did she stop to rest, nor did she ever complain.

For three hours they'd toiled in the scorching late afternoon as it dwindled to twilight sun. He was going to die.

"Well, I guess you're not used to hard work," she said, straightening up, which made him a little regretful, because if nothing else had been pleasant about this outing she'd talked him into, staring at her perky little buns had been. She had great legs—even if they weren't long like a model's—and a great posterior. Quite a compact little woman. "Better take you in before you get sick on me."

"All I feel is hot and tired." He wouldn't admit for a million dollars—which he didn't have, anyway—that he'd sort of enjoyed working with her. She was quiet when she was working, her movements efficient. It wasn't actually all that hot. Now that the sun had nearly slipped away, the breeze had picked up nicely. He couldn't remember the last time he'd spent so much time that wasn't sexual or self-serving with a woman.

"Well, come on." She dusted off her legs. "Let's get you a drink."

"Beer, I hope."

"Don't have any," she said on a laugh. "Iced tea is about all this gal keeps."

"Don't drink?"

She shrugged as she walked toward the house. "When it's hot I'd just as soon drink something non-alcoholic."

"I'll take tea right now and not gripe."

"You mean it?" She looked over her shoulder at him as she walked down an evenly spaced row. "It's not a fancy blend, I warn you."

"Very funny." The woman made a sport out of

poking fun at him. Well, he had news for her: he could get along just fine without designer-label tea. But he was proud of his Ferrari, and she could just quit harping on that one. "Maybe I should check in with the garage and see if they've had a chance to look at my car."

"Help yourself." She pulled open the screen door, not waiting for him to walk in behind her. He scrambled to catch the door, then watched her walk toward the kitchen. A moment later she put a glass of tea on a side table in the dining room where he hovered. "There's your drink. The phone's in the kitchen. I'm going upstairs."

"Thanks." He drank every drop as he watched Dixie's cute little bottom shift from side to side as she ascended the stairs. Shaking his head, he tore his gaze away, instantly seeing Rascal sitting at his feet like a giant feather duster-mop combination. "What do you want, hound?"

The dog wagged its plumed tail patiently, its mouth open in a toothy dog smile.

"Well, go on. Your mistress went that way. Whatever you want, I don't have it." He shooed the animal, but it didn't budge.

"He wants a piece of ice out of your glass!" Dixie hollered down the stairs.

"Ice?" Garrison stared at the dog. "Oh, come on. I'm not—you don't want this, do you?" He shook his glass, making the cubes tinkle. The dog sat straighter in anticipation. "I'm not giving you any," he whispered so that Dixie couldn't hear. "You can just take your hairiness elsewhere."

Rascal inched forward to sit on his foot.

"You're getting more hair on me than the last

blonde I went out with!'' Garrison moved back. "Go away!''

The dog rose up, carefully putting two paws on Garrison's shirtfront so that he could lick the cool glass he was clutching.

"All right! Get down, you great beast!'' He pushed the large dog with an impatient hand. "Dixie!'' he yelled, greatly unnerved. "Your dog is attacking me!''

"Give him the ice!''

"How?'' At this point, he would have given him an iceberg to save his own limbs. But he wasn't about to let those pointy teeth get near his hand, if that's what Dixie had in mind.

"Garrison! Just toss a piece onto the floor, for heaven's sake!''

Quickly, he dug out a chunk and tossed it into the next room. Rascal went bounding after the ice, skidding on the hardwood floors as he made his capture. Satisfied crunching told Garrison he wasn't the only body in the room that had suffered from a few hours in the heat. "Oh, for the love of Mike,'' he grumbled. "I'm not cut out for this kind of existence.'' Ice-devouring, seventy-pound beasts ranked low on his list of things to acquire, as in: would never make it on his list at all.

Dixie came down the stairs at that moment, barefoot. Her hair was neatly combed and her face moist from a rinsing. She'd put a light pink lipstick on, and shorts that were pink-candy colored. The sleeveless white eyelet blouse had a scoop neck, so that when she leaned over to pet Rascal, he got an unexpected and delicious view of her not-D-cups.

"Oh, good boy,'' he told Rascal sincerely. "I take back everything uncomplimentary I said about you.''

Chapter Thirteen

"Did you say bad things to Rascal?" Dixie straightened, looking at Garrison with a half smile he found as sexy as her bouncing ponytail.

"I may have intimated that he wasn't welcome to shed on me." Garrison didn't want to talk about that right now. "Of course, I didn't take it too personally. He is a dog, after all."

"Not just a dog," Dixie disagreed, hugging her Rascal around the neck. Garrison could only wish for such affection to be showered on him. "He's the man of the house, aren't you, boy?"

Rascal grinned up at Garrison, enjoying the fact that his mistress was giving him all her attention.

"Did you make your phone call?"

Garrison shook his head. "I—no, actually. Somehow, I forgot about it."

"Forgot about your Ferrari?" She clicked her tongue against her teeth. "I can hardly believe that."

"Me, either." He refused to think about what might have swept his brain clean of his passion for his chickmobile. "Are you ready to release me? Have you extracted a gas tank's wages from me so I can go home?"

She cocked her head at him. "Do you want to go home?"

Her question caught him off guard. "Well, I...now that you ask, not especially."

"I've got some chicken you're welcome to grill. If you can," she hastened to add.

"Dixie, I can light a grill."

She beamed, as if pleased by the knowledge that he was good for something. This goaded him into attempting to change her image of him. "As a matter of fact, I can open a bottle of wine without damaging myself with the corkscrew, I can set a table without suffering cutlery wounds and I can wash dishes without drowning. Impressed?"

"Absolutely," she said, mock seriously. "Do show me."

"I'll show you something I've been wanting to show you for a long time." He reached out and took her wrist, pulling her toward him. She came willingly, and he slid one hand behind her neck, the other at her waist. Ever so slowly, he joined his lips to hers, feeling shock run through him like cold water.

She felt like heaven.

He kissed her like there was no tomorrow, and when they both ran out of breath a moment later, he drew back regretfully.

She stared up into his eyes. "Is that what you wanted to show me?" she whispered. "That you're a great kisser?"

"Nah. I wanted to show you how much I think I like you." He ran one finger along her cheek, almost surprised at his words.

"Really?" Light-paprika-colored eyebrows soared above her incredible tourmaline eyes.

"I'm afraid so." He was drawn to her lips again, kissing her like he was starved for the taste of her. Dixie moaned softly, and Garrison thought he would die of want. Gently he pulled away, running his hands down her arms until they finally separated from each other at the fingertips. "Maybe you ought to show me where the grill is so I can get to work on dinner."

"Okay. And since you claim you can open a bottle of wine without hurting yourself," she reminded him with a sweet smile, "I'm going to hold you to that. I've got something to show you after dinner, Mr. Ferrari, and I want you in one piece."

He wanted to wag like Rascal. By golly, the woman wanted him.

If he had anything to do with it, she was going to have him.

PARKER GOT UP to check on Meg, but she was sound asleep in the room across the hall. Going to church and then having a pony ride had certainly tuckered her out. Noreen slept soundly, as well, her long blond hair adorning the pillow next to his. He sighed, rubbing the back of his neck. The woman had no idea what she did to him. It was all he could do not to ravish her.

In the end that would get them nowhere. She had real hesitation about a serious commitment to him, and he couldn't blame her. She didn't believe in love at first sight. He hadn't in a long time. Lavinia had just about cured him of that.

But he'd taken one look at Noreen in Rockwall's town square and known he couldn't let her walk away. Then he'd kissed her—and lost his heart.

If Noreen had been skittish about him before, Lavinia's sudden appearance hadn't helped matters. He sighed heavily. The best thing he could do was call his ex-wife and see what she wanted to talk about. He went downstairs and found the phone, dialing her parents' number.

After speaking to her mother for a moment, he asked for Lavinia. In a second she was on the line.

"Hello, Parker."

"Hi." He checked his watch. "I won't be able to make it back into Dallas as early as I thought I would."

"So you won't…be coming by." Her tone was disconsolate.

"No. How long are you in town? I can bring Meg by another time," he offered, trying to reassure her that he had no intention of not letting her see Meg to her heart's content while she was visiting her folks.

"Well, I really wanted to see you." She was quiet for a second, before almost shyly saying, "I was serious earlier, Parker. I want to talk about our marriage."

"What about it?" It was over, had been over. What was there to talk about?

"This is hard. I'd hoped we could speak face-to-face…"

"I'll be in Dallas too late tonight to come by." *If* Noreen wanted him to stay that long with her, and he hoped she did. "Tomorrow, if you want, we could meet at a McDonald's for lunch. Meg can play on the toys."

There was a long silence on the other end. "That wasn't exactly what I had in mind."

"What did you have in mind?" He was finished with the guessing game. Lavinia was hard to pin down about most things, but right now, he didn't want to play. He wanted to get back upstairs to Noreen, and wake her up with a bad knock-knock joke whispered in her ear, just to stay true to the Texas tall tale they'd been swapping.

"I want to come back home," Lavinia said, interrupting his pleasant daydream of slowly waking Noreen with lots of kisses.

"Back home?" he echoed, frowning.

"To you. To Meg. To our family. I want to be the wife to you that I wasn't before, Parker."

He briefly wondered about the artsy Romeo she'd left him to find herself with. "Lavinia, listen. Our marriage was over too long ago for me to even take you seriously now. I'm not trying to be cruel. But I just don't see us as an option anymore."

"You mean you've met someone else." Her statement was flat, her tone chagrined.

"Did you expect that after our divorce I'd still be hanging on to the hope that you'd return to Meg and me?"

"Calendar years can't measure love, Parker. Love is an unquantifiable emotion. It transcends time, place and human consciousness."

He rolled his eyes. "Guess I'm still too uptight to get it, Lavinia. Sorry."

"Oh, Parker, you're not uptight, not really. I've missed your steadfastness."

Now he was steadfast. Sheesh. He wondered if Lavinia had always viewed him like some kind of unattractive rock formation that time hadn't quite mellowed into an acceptable shape for landscaping. *I haven't missed your flakiness,* he thought, but he would never say that to a woman he'd promised to love. She was Meg's mother, and they would always have that bond. It would hurt Meg if her parents didn't get along, artsy Romeos notwithstanding. "Lavinia, listen, I've got to go. We can discuss anything you like later, but…this particular thing you're alluding to isn't going to happen. I'm sorry."

She was silent. "It's serious, isn't it? You and the woman with the pretty shoes Meg was wearing."

"It is for me. I'm sorry." He sighed, hating to hurt Lavinia, as much as he doubted her sincerity.

"Well, I guess that's all there is to say, then."

"I guess so. I'll bring Meg by your folks' tomorrow."

The line clicked, signaling that she'd hung up. Parker shook his head. Not a word of apology, really, for leaving him with a small child. For leaving him at all, for no better reason than her own selfish whim. He wished he'd realized Lavinia was that self-centered.

He stopped that thought immediately. If he hadn't fallen in love with Lavinia, he wouldn't have Meg now. And that was reason enough not to wish to turn the clock backward in time.

But he could go forward. There was a woman upstairs who wasn't immature in the least. Noreen was responsible and warm and salt of the earth. California's free-spirit communities would never be her destination, but maybe he could talk her into Paris for a honeymoon.

He obviously had to figure out how to tell a better knock-knock joke. But Lavinia was right about one thing: he did tend to be, well, not uptight, exactly. He preferred to think of it as consistent. Methodical. Predictable, in an unpredictable world.

Maybe he *was* boring, like she'd intimated when she left.

And maybe he was too scared to make love to Noreen for fear of what had happened with Lavinia. He'd fallen in love, they'd made love—with all the youthful enthusiasm of twenty-somethings—and found themselves at the altar with starry-eyed optimism.

But who was to say that had been wrong? People changed. There were no guarantees.

Unless he chose someone this time who was more like him; more balanced, more predictable.

Noreen wasn't boring, though. She made him want to buy out a Victoria's Secret lingerie store down to those silly padded hangers just so he could see her in something luscious and sexy every night.

He ran up the stairs, checking swiftly on his sleeping daughter before locking the door and diving in bed next to Noreen.

"Knock-knock," he whispered into her ear.

"Who's there?" she mumbled.

"Daddy Charming."

"Daddy Charming who?"

"Daddy Charming the pants off of you."

Noreen opened her eyes. "That's so corny it's bad." But she smiled, and he smiled back.

"Well, maybe it's not funny, but I meant it."

Her eyes widened. "It's not a joke?"

"Uh-uh." He nuzzled into the curve of her neck and slipped one hand around her waist to her backside. "It's more of a mission statement."

"It's your mission to get my pants off?" She ran one hand through his hair. "I thought—"

He interrupted her with a breath-stealing kiss. "It's

my most necessary mission to make love to you. If you accept this mission, you will probably be in danger.''

She laughed. "Of what?"

"Of finding yourself the victim of my uncontrollable desire for you."

"Really?" She looked fascinated as she began unbuttoning his shirt. "Uncontrollable?"

He nodded, doing the same to her buttons. "Uncontrollable. Fierce. Can't wait another second."

"Oh, my." She reached for the button on his chinos, then slid the zipper down. "I hope I'm prepared for this."

"I am. I hope you won't be offended, but…" He reached for his wallet after they scooched his trousers down. "After I met you, I decided it was high time to hit the drugstore counter to reacquaint myself with the new approach to the age-old protection device. And, man, is it more of a dilemma than ever. You can get blue or plaid or spiked and ribbed." Extracting his wallet, he pulled out a condom, which he held by one end so it could accordion down into a line of ten. "Now, granted, I can't use all of these this afternoon—Meg will probably wake up at any time— but it's my sincere hope that by the end of this supply, I'll be able to get a yes out of you." He kissed her long and slow. "Or at least a maybe and another box."

She giggled as he tossed the pants to the floor and the condoms onto the nightstand. "I'll have to make you wait for my answer until after the first of those um, packages."

He unclasped her bra, removing it with slow hands. "I'll be very gentle," he whispered, all trace of laughter gone now. She was so beautiful. Her breasts were round and firm, just as sexy as he could ever imagine. He took a nipple in his mouth, feeling himself harden at her moan. Lingering strokes along her waist seemed to relax her, so he kissed down her stomach to her navel, gently easing her pants to her ankles, where he left butterfly-soft kisses. Then he kissed his way back up her calves to her thighs, to where he could taste the womanliness inside her.

"Oh, my gosh," she whispered. Her hands tangled in his hair, pulling him back up so that she could kiss him. Parker took her lips slowly, all the while stroking her nipples and the flat of her stomach, back up to her nipples, which had peaked tight. Before he realized it, she had wrapped one small hand around him, hesitantly exploring his maleness. He stilled, almost stunned by her touch. She sighed, and he couldn't stand it any longer. With two fingers, he stroked along her inner core, feeling her slickness and the intriguing hardness her softness hid. She began moving against his hand, and he stroked faster, knowing intuitively what she wanted. He put his lips to her breast, catching a nipple between his teeth in a gentle nip, then moved to the other one, all the while stroking her.

"Oh, oh, oh!" she cried suddenly. "Oh, Parker!"

He waited, lightly stroking her, until she had relaxed a little. Then he positioned himself, gently sliding inside her, filling her with the aching hardness he needed to join to her at that soul-deep connection.

Her eyes flew open at the unexpected sensation of pain. "Oh, my goodness. Ouch."

"I'm sorry," he whispered. "I'll make it as easy as possible."

"I'm not sure you're really hurting me." She

reached up to clasp him to her, and as Parker reveled in the closeness between them, he realized he'd forgotten the condom.

"Uh, knock-knock," he whispered into her ear.

"Who's there?" She stroked his back with light fingertips.

"Forgotta."

"Forgotta who?"

"Forgotta put the raincoat on and there's a fierce storm brewing."

She ran her hands over his buttocks. "My family has always cautioned me about going out in the rain without proper gear."

"I would tell Meg the same thing. My apologies for the delay." He withdrew regretfully and reached for the package.

"Let me. If you can figure out how to saddle Meanie, I bet I can do this." She took the package and tore it open, pulling out the ringed latex. Sitting up, she squinted at it, then glanced between his legs with concern. "Um, I don't think you bought a big enough condom."

He took her hands in his, guiding her fingers to roll the device down over his hardness. "It accommodates."

"Amazing," she said, her expression awed but not nervous, as she stroked him around and beneath the condom's edge. He hissed with unexpected pleasure. She pulled him back to her as she reclined again, taking him between her hands to lead him where he wanted most to be. "What will they ever think of next?"

"Maybe a condom that beeps if you forget to put

it on.'' He slid inside her again, feeling like he would climax on contact. ''Did I hurt you?''

''No,'' she whispered, arching against him. ''Whatever you're doing, don't stop.''

He moved to the rhythm that she set. She slipped satiny thighs around him, urging him faster, and Parker wondered if he could hold on. The pleasure was closing in on him. He commanded himself to wait, trying not to concentrate on the feel of Noreen under him, her body matching his in motion. They fit together perfectly. She was the right woman for him, whether he'd convinced her of that or not. *I will,* he promised himself.

She cried out in sudden wonder, clutching his shoulders. He squeezed his eyes shut, feeling her tightness surround him. It was all he could take, and he cried out with his own climax, slumping against her in absolute wonder at the immense pleasure.

As his racing heartbeat subsided, he kissed her temple, then her lips. ''Are you all right?''

''Mmm.'' She had a slight smile on her face. ''You?''

Wrapping his arms around her tightly and tucking her up against him, Parker said, ''I don't know how I could feel any better.''

She tucked herself up under his chin. ''Me, either. If this is a dream, I don't ever want to wake up.''

He didn't, either.

''How much longer will Meg nap?''

Squinting out the window, he saw that the sky was casting shadows of nightfall over the descending sun. ''I should go get her up. Otherwise, she won't sleep tonight.''

But he didn't move, and a few seconds later, they'd both drifted off to sleep in each other's arms, content.

NOREEN NOTICED, a while later, when Parker pulled away from her, but she wasn't ready to open her eyes yet. She was still under the heavenly spell of their lovemaking. She listened to the sounds of him getting dressed, then heard the door open. *In a moment, I'll get up and join them,* she told herself. *We can grill the hamburgers I've got in the freezer.*

A few moments later she heard a car start. Jumping from the bed, she glanced out her window. Parker's Mercedes was heading down the road. Her heart sank. How could he just leave like that?

More than crushed, she pulled on clean jeans and a shirt, smoothing her long blond hair back with a headband. It wasn't like him to be ungentlemanly. She'd wanted to say goodbye to him and to Meg. Quickly, she made the bed and went downstairs.

A note lay propped on the kitchen table. "Meg and I have gone into town to get some Dumpy's Fried Chicken for dinner—if you'll have us. And do they sell champagne in this town on Sunday? RSVP my car phone."

Her heart soared as she dialed the number he'd written.

He answered on the first ring.

"I've got a bottle here," she said without preamble. "Left over from one of the aunt's wedding showers. Their secret recipe for the most popular parties in Rockwall is to spike their champagne with a smidgen of fruit punch. They've always got plenty on hand. I'll put it in the fridge."

"We're not overstaying our welcome?"

She smiled into the phone. "Hurry back," she told him. "I'm hungry."

Her tone implied she was hungry for him. "You have no idea how delighted I am to hear it. If I pick up extra chicken for the aunts, do you think they can be talked into eating dinner with us?"

She was touched by his thoughtfulness. "I know they're on tenterhooks hoping for an invitation. And tell Meg I've got something special planned for her tonight."

"I will." He was quiet for a moment. "Thanks, Noreen. I appreciate you thinking of her."

It was impossible not to think of that adorable child and her wonderful, considerate father. "Well, I'm an excellent businesswoman. Two for the price of one is a deal I couldn't pass up."

He laughed. "We'll be right back."

Noreen hung up the phone, feeling happiness cloud around her like starry mists. She'd never dreamed love could feel so good. She couldn't imagine anything ever spoiling the way she felt right now.

"WELL, THE MERCEDES just vacated the premises." Hattie lowered her binoculars in disappointment.

"Quit spying!" Priscilla snapped. The three women were grouped over at Hattie's because it was middle ground—and because she had the only set of decent binoculars.

"I was hoping he'd stay until dinner," Charlene said quietly. "I made up a three-bean salad in case Noreen called."

"I thought the purpose of our spying was to make certain we didn't intrude upon any private moments between Parker and Noreen, which would preclude dinner, I should think," Priscilla observed.

"It doesn't matter. We weren't invited." Hattie put the binoculars back to her face. "Although I had planned on seeing if Parker would let me bring Meg back over here to play so they could go out on a date. I doubt he would," she murmured, "but I am so anxious to hug that little girl." Straining to see beyond the limit of the binoculars—dratted things weren't capable of right angles so she could see the entire front yard—Hattie frowned. "I wonder what Garrison is up to. He's been gone an awfully long time. Mischief, I'm certain."

"Maybe he's looking for a job," Charlene said.

Hattie and Priscilla both turned to favor her with an immediate frown. The phone rang, making all three of them jump guiltily. Hattie put the binoculars down and skittered to the phone. "Hello?" she said innocently. "Oh, Garrison. Oh. That's too bad. I see. Well, okay. Thank you for calling."

She replaced the phone, her mouth open with shock. "I don't know what to say."

"Skip the drama and tell us who it was," Priscilla demanded.

"It was Garrison," she said in amazement. "His Ferrari broke down, so Dixie picked him up. He was calling to let us know he wouldn't be home for dinner."

Her two sisters were agog. "Was he drunk?" Charlene wondered.

"Or at knifepoint?" Priscilla theorized. "For that boy to have developed manners, he had to have been in a very unusual situation."

"Dixie wouldn't hold Garrison captive," Charlene warbled, shocked. "She's such a sweet girl."

"Yes, but she has the Adams determination, and that apple didn't fall too far from Ned's family tree." Hattie knew all about Adams determination. Ned had been determined to get Hattie to the altar for ages, and she'd only been able to fend him off with her own considerable will—and a lot of phony-baloney excuses. Which he'd outwaited with dogged purpose, a trait she secretly admired. Nothing was worth having if it wasn't worth the wait.

But if Dixie was hoping to get Garrison to the altar, it probably would be at knifepoint—even Hattie's magic wand appeared to have run out of steam where that boy was concerned.

"HOLD STILL!" Garrison commanded Rascal. "Dammit, beast!"

Dixie laughed. "Rascal, get down!" She rescued Garrison, waved the dog out of the kitchen and went back to cutting country-fresh tomatoes. "He's very protective, and you moved too fast to suit him," she explained. "That's why he jumped up on you. For some reason, I think Rascal feels you're not quite trustworthy."

Garrison wiped his brow and went back to washing lettuce. "I'm convinced he thinks I'm going to be one of his table scraps."

"No. He's not allowed to have people food. It's not healthy."

He glanced at Dixie competently cutting vegetables on the wooden chopping board. It was amazing how well the two of them fit in this tiny kitchen even with a dog jumping up to rest his paws on Garrison's back.

And the beast was smart: Garrison *had* been eyeing Dixie with a glance that was just short of starving.

The dog wasn't smart enough for Garrison, though. Tonight the bedroom door was going to be locked, and the collie was going to be on the other side. "You fed him ice."

"You can't really consider that food." She shrugged and reached for an onion. "It's hot out. Besides, he likes ice."

Garrison liked anything cool that melted in his arms, something he was going to achieve with Dixie very soon. He'd better call Noreen, as he had the aunts, and tell her not to expect him. "I'm going to use your phone one more time."

"Calling the repair shop?" she asked with a smile.

"My sister." He walked over to the phone. When Noreen answered, he said, "It's Garrison. I just wanted to let you know I'll be out late."

"Okay." Noreen sounded faintly surprised to hear from him, but then said, "The shop called. Your repairs should run around five thousand dollars."

"Five thousand bucks!" he hollered into the phone. Rascal jumped up on him, placing paws on his chest so that he could sniff his face warily. "That car is practically new!" Or at least his gambling buddy had claimed it was. He hadn't checked the story or the car out too well in his zeal to own a Ferrari at a price he thought he could manage.

"I'm sorry, Garrison." Noreen actually did sound regretful and sympathetic. "Maybe you should talk to the mechanic. He might have had the wrong car, because I'm certain he called it a heap of junk."

His blood pressure exploded. "A heap of—"

Rascal leaped up again, his paws landing squarely on Garrison's chest.

"Get down, Rascal!" Dixie forced her dog down with an apologetic gaze at Garrison. He didn't care about Rascal's bad manners, though, because with Dixie bent over her dog, he could definitely enjoy the cleavage show. His mouth watered so that he nearly missed Noreen's next words.

"And a Jefferson Crower of Crower Real Estate called about some property you wanted to talk to him about."

He could hear the accusation in Noreen's tone. What did she have to be disappointed about? It was his land, damn it, and he had a five-thousand-buck repair bill on his beloved Ferrari, not to mention that time was ticking down on the money he owed for the vehicle itself.

He was in deep, deep trouble.

"I'll call him back," Garrison said curtly. "Thanks, Noreen."

Hanging up, he hesitated, foundering when Dixie turned her pretty, freckle-dusted face toward him as she patted Rascal. "Everything all right?"

No. It wasn't. He was caught between two worlds, and the sensation was frightening. She reached to brush her hand against her hip, a gesture that drew his eye to her adorable fanny. What was he doing in this doll's house? Especially with a mangy dog running his chops over him like Garrison was a human steak bone, while he played Farmer Joe with Farmer Jane who turned into Motorcycle Mama when she left her field-hidden hut? He'd been in mansions where the bathrooms were bigger than Dixie's dwelling.

He swallowed, his throat tight. "I have to make one more call. This one's a bit private."

"A woman?" she teased.

"No." But he didn't elaborate.

Some of the shine left her eyes. "In my bedroom. Help yourself."

"Thanks." He left the kitchen and headed up the narrow stairs. There was one bedroom on the left, and one on the right which had been converted into a sewing room. One bathroom at the end of the small hall finished off the upstairs. Garrison could feel the walls closing in on him.

He went into what was obviously Dixie's bedroom. His throat dried out instantly. White lace curtains hung at two windows. Happy-faced dolls lay across lace-tipped pillowcases in a casual tea party. A pink scarf adorned a small lamp. The room smelled just like her, light and feminine and fresh. A white old-fashioned phone sat on the round nightstand next to her bed, so Garrison seated himself next to a Raggedy Ann as he reached for the phone, his hand suddenly arrested in midair.

She'd drawn hearts on a pad next to the phone. Encircled by one of the hearts was the name *Garrison*, in lovely scrolling letters. The shock of seeing it there made him snatch the pad up for closer inspection. He felt harder hit than when he'd heard about the Ferrari bill—a much more devastating impact. His name had never looked so nice before, so special. Strangely, he felt important. *The woman thinks about me when she's in this frilly closet!*

A pang hit his chest around the region of his heart. Dixie was never going to understand! As much as he wanted her more than anything he'd ever wanted before, he had to talk to Jefferson Crower.

That would take his name right out of her heart, he was certain. Instantly a disastrous feeling struck him. He really was in deep, deep trouble.

It might be *his* heart that ended up broken.

Chapter Fourteen

"Hooray! We've been invited to dinner, girls!" Hattie crowed that same night. She put down the phone and bustled to lock the back door. "Get your three-bean salad, Charlene. We get to see that sweet little girl!"

"Do you think we ought to?" Priscilla looked worried. "Maybe we ought to leave Noreen and Parker alone so they can get to know each other better. I'm sure they don't need a bunch of old ladies hanging around."

"Old!" Hattie waved that off. "We're energetic and useful! Besides which," she said with a cagey gleam in her eye, "couldn't they get to know each other a lot better if we offered to keep an eye on Meg for a while?"

"That makes sense." Charlene nodded and headed out to retrieve her salad.

"All right." Priscilla still didn't look certain.

"And all the better because Garrison's hung up with Dixie. What a good girl she is, keeping him out of our hair." Hattie grabbed some potato salad out of the fridge. She'd prepared it just in case such an invitation came their way.

"Are we walking?" Priscilla asked.

"Parker's coming to get us. Finally we get to ride in that wonderful car of his." Hattie beamed. "I like Ned's truck, but Parker's Mercedes is studly, you've got to admit."

"Oh, for heaven's sake!"

Priscilla slammed the front door as she headed to her place, bringing back a plate of deviled eggs a few moments later. Parker pulled up about the time she reached Hattie's porch, so the three of them waited with their plates of goodies.

"Hi!" he called over the top of the hood.

"Tell me he is not the most devastating piece of eye candy your eyes ever did see," Hattie murmured for only Priscilla and Charlene to hear.

Her sisters sighed in exasperation, but Hattie didn't care. She knew a good thing when she saw it, and fortunately it appeared that Noreen did, too.

"I CAN'T FATHOM what's gotten into Garrison myself," Noreen admitted to Hattie. "He actually called to tell me he'd be home late."

"He called us, too."

Noreen shook her head, a trifle worried. "To be honest, I thought he'd only called to get his messages. The man Parker outbid for Mrs. Martin's land left a message for Garrison."

Hattie stared up at her tall goddaughter. "Why would he do that?"

"I suppose Garrison called him."

"Uh-oh." Hattie sighed. "I do wonder if that boy will ever make something of himself." She laid the eggs and salad on the table, then returned to the kitchen. "Noreen, did you ever think that maybe Garrison has a good idea?"

"What?" Noreen nearly dropped the plate she was carrying. "What are you talking about?"

"That maybe the farm takes up too much of your life." Hattie stared at her with sincere eyes. "You should have a family, honey. A husband. Children. You've shouldered all of us for a long time. Now it should be your turn."

"Absolutely not. No way." She couldn't give up the only way of life she'd ever known! She'd gone to college for this. Her daddy had loved this farm. Together they had shared a bond watching sun and rain nourish the plants, while at night the moon kept silent vigil over the land that held their dreams.

"You wouldn't vote your shares with Garrison to maneuver me into marrying Parker, would you, Aunt Hattie?" she asked suspiciously. "I don't mind a little help in my personal life, but I'd consider that interference of the worst sort. *If* he ever proposed to me, I'd want it to be something he thought of, not an idea you'd helped him into thinking."

"Goodness, no! But now that you bring him up, what about Parker? If he proposed, of course," she amended hastily.

"He hasn't said he has a problem with farming. In fact, he seems to think this is a good place for Meg, if..."

"If?" Hattie prodded.

"Well, if we were to develop into a serious relationship." Noreen wasn't about to encourage Hattie's well-meaning prying.

"You of all people know how much time you spend in the fields. What about Meg?"

Noreen's hands stilled over the chicken she was unwrapping. Meg deserved a mother who spent time with her. Parker said his ex-wife hadn't devoted much of her time to Meg. It would be unfair for the child to suffer that fate a second time. "I don't know," she murmured. "I guess I was going along so much in the moment that I didn't think the whole thing through."

"I'm not saying there's a problem. And I'm never going to suggest that Garrison is right about anything. But it's given me pause," Hattie admitted. "Meg would have us, naturally. But then there are bake sales, ballet lessons, PTA meetings, and—" She met Noreen's troubled gaze. "It's just something to keep in mind."

"I don't think it has to be Parker *or* the farm." Noreen felt very defensive about the situation.

"No, I'm not saying it does. I'm saying you don't have to stay here forever because of us, honey."

"I'm here because I want to be." She put the chicken on a platter and carried it to the dining room. "The three of you are not a burden to me. Nor would Parker and Meg be."

"And I reckon Parker hopes you feel that way, or he wouldn't be sitting at your table, devouring you with his eyes. You don't make a move that he doesn't notice, you know. The man is smitten!"

"Oh, Aunt Hattie." Noreen couldn't deny the pleasure that thought brought her. But she also couldn't deny that there was a lot she had to think about where her future was concerned. For the first year since she'd taken over running the farm, she stood a real shot at a bumper harvest. Her pumpkins were shaping up nicely, and decorated a wide expanse of field. Between this crop and her two others, harvest time was going to be fifteen-hour days. But she couldn't sell the land around her home, even though it would mean more time to be a wife and mother. Nor would she want Garrison to sell out his percentage...because the land had been her father's, and selling might bring development right to her door.

The perfect solution would be for her to buy Garrison out. Maybe after the pumpkin crop was harvested, she could. It was the only extra profit crop she had. Strictly speaking, half of the proceeds should be Garrison's, but maybe she could talk him into letting her make a couple of instalment payments with her portion.

But that didn't solve the part of the puzzle Parker and Meg had become in her life. *I can think about this later,* she told herself, completely aware that Parker's gaze followed her as she set a tea pitcher on the table near him. Her body tingled with excitement as he reached out to squeeze her hand, making her remember the wonderful feeling of being in his arms.

Like Meg, he deserved a better fate the second time around.

She had a lot of thinking to do.

NOREEN KISSED her relatives good-night after a wonderful evening watching Meg hunt in the front yard for faux arrowheads that were spray-painted different colors. The child had been absolutely fascinated by the idea of her own treasure excavation, and Noreen's heart had expanded to painful proportions watching the little girl happily collecting her goodies in a plastic pail.

It would be almost impossible not to fall in love

with Meg. The card deck had been stacked against Noreen ever since Hattie had concocted her impulsive matchmaking. Her gaze slid to Parker, who kissed each lady's cheek with affection. *It could be like this for always,* she thought with sudden wonder.

"Noreen, I'm going to drive them home," Parker said. "It's not right for three lovely women to walk so far in the dark, and Meg will enjoy the ride."

"We walk all the time. It's beneficial," Hattie told him.

"Allow me the courtesy of chivalry." He shooed them toward his car. "I'll be right back to help with the dishes."

"I'll stay with Miss Noreen, Daddy," Meg said in her piping, sweet voice.

"Okay, sweetheart." He waved and got in the car.

Meg looked up at Noreen. "Am I going to spend the night again tonight?"

The dark, shiny waves of hair surrounding the heart-shaped face stole Noreen's love right out of the protective place she'd been trying to hoard it. She gathered Meg into her lap. "I think your dad said he had to get back to Dallas tonight."

The child nodded wisely. "To see my mother."

"I...I think maybe that's the case." Noreen wasn't sure. What she was certain of was that the knowledge would hurt. It shouldn't. But suddenly she was aware of an emotion she'd never felt before. She wished Parker and Meg were her family. Her protective instincts surged. *I would never give up such a wonderful miracle.*

"I wish you could be my mother," Meg said, her face plaintive. "But I already have one."

Noreen swallowed. "I know." But she tucked Meg into her lap more securely, hugging her tight.

"Maybe you could be my second mother. Maybe I could have two!" Meg said, her voice lifting. "Daddy never tells me no about anything—well, not much—so maybe I could ask him!"

"Oh, Meg." The hope in the little girl's tone had been heart stealing. Noreen felt as if Parker were bearing the blame for something she'd done. But she couldn't tell Meg that.

"Would you like to be my second mother?"

Noreen stared into the child's eyes. "I—yes. But—"

"Then I'll ask Daddy." Meg leaned back against Noreen, confident that she'd get her way. "I've been wishing you could, every night."

Noreen breathed in a deep sigh. It wasn't that simple, of course. She couldn't become a stepmother just because Meg wished it.

"Miss Noreen, I want some clothes like you wear."

She glanced at Meg's pretty Sunday dress. The child was always dressed like a princess. "Why do you want jeans, honey?"

"I want to be like you," she replied simply. "Wanna see my hopper?" Her attention was now solely on her plastic pail.

Noreen leaned to see what a hopper was. Inside the bucket, a tiny brown and green grasshopper jumped around on top of the arrowheads. "Oh, that's nice, Meg," she praised. "A grasshopper."

"Yes. My very own." She set the pail in her lap and beamed at her new pet. Noreen leaned back, sighing as she stared at the chubby-cheeked, delightful child. Hattie was worried about Meg's future, as well she should be. Dating a sexy single dad was all very exciting—but Noreen was growing terribly attached to his daughter, too. It made resisting their pull all that much more difficult.

Parker came in the front door, smiling at them as they sat on the bottom stair. "What are you two doing?"

Meg looked up instantly. "Daddy, my hoppergrass and I want to stay with Miss Noreen."

He smiled at Noreen. "We have to go home tonight, Meg."

"She says she wants us to stay. It's okay, Daddy."

Squatting down next to his daughter, Parker tweaked one of her curls. "Miss Noreen's a nice lady, honey. But we can't just move in with her."

"Yes, we can, Daddy. Miss Noreen is going to be my second mother."

His gaze ricocheted to Noreen. "She is?"

Noreen shrugged helplessly. "The conversation got a bit out of my hands."

"Can she convince you of what I couldn't? Should I have utilized this strategy previously?"

She shook her head. "Parker—"

"Okay." He stood, tugging at one of his daughter's curls. "Let's help clean up. You can dry the forks, honey."

Meg ran into the kitchen, taking her pail with her. Noreen started to follow, but Parker caught her by the arm, gently turning her toward him. He kissed her slowly, once on the lips, and then moved to her cheek. They stood there together for a long moment, Noreen's heart beating like she'd been sprinting.

"If you ever change your mind, we'd love for you to accept. I know you think I only want you for Meg's sake, but after today, I believe you know there's more to it than that.''

She closed her eyes, trying to fight Parker's appeal. "I know." She leaned into his warmth. "Your daughter wants a pair of blue jeans."

"She does?" He sounded astonished.

"Yes. She says she wants to look like me."

"Well, hey, that's not a bad goal." He gave her a gentle squeeze. "I never thought about buying her jeans. Little girls wear dresses. But the way she got down on the ground hunting arrowheads tells me she'd be a lot more comfortable if she did dress like you. See what a good example you are for us?" he murmured against her hair.

His tone was light, but Noreen couldn't be.

"I wasn't looking for anything like this to happen in my life," she said shakily. "I think that's what's got me thrown a little. I'm used to relying on myself. Suddenly I've got the chance for something I never knew I could have, and I think…maybe I'm a little nervous. I'm not very experienced at love, you know."

He rubbed her shoulders. "I'm not very experienced at love myself. This time around, it feels much more…real. Mature. Wonderful."

She looked up at him shyly. "I'm glad."

"No one's rushing you, Noreen. I'm not surprised Meg wants to keep you, though." He kissed her temple, and ran a hand down her long hair. "I would promise not to be a pumpkin-eater kind of husband, Noreen."

"What does that mean?" she asked, laughing.

"Hey, I read nursery rhymes to my daughter. You

know the pumpkin-eating guy who had a wife and couldn't keep her, so he incarcerated her inside one?''

Noreen smiled at him inquisitively. "I think I've heard of that unfortunate couple."

He pulled her to him. "You've got that field of pumpkins out there, you know. Maybe you're worried I'll try to stick you in a shell. But I think," he said, stealing a kiss, "that if I can trust you not to ditch me and Meg, you can trust me not to tie you down. We've both got something at stake here."

"I know." She stole a kiss of her own. "I'm not worried about being tied down at all." Maybe his ex-wife hadn't wanted to be with him and Meg, but Noreen would take her commitment seriously. He wouldn't need a shell to keep her very well—if she could allow herself to make that move. "It's unnerving, isn't it? Learning to let someone in your life?"

"It is." He tucked her head under his chin. "I'm going to have to learn to like pumpkin pie."

"You will when you taste mine."

"Daddy!" Meg called, poking her head around the kitchen door. "You're 'posed to be cleaning. Kissin's for afterward!"

Noreen pulled away from Parker. "You've taught her to be so responsible," she said with a smile.

"Too much so," he said on a groan. "I wanted to talk some more about your pie."

"Come on." She took him by the hand and pulled him toward the kitchen. "Kissin's for afterward."

GARRISON could hardly eat the dinner he and Dixie had prepared. He'd completely lost his appetite. She was staring at him with those trusting eyes, and he felt ill. He'd called Jefferson Crower, but he was worried. He had a lot on his mind. Maybe he should just ask Dixie to take him home.

"If you're finished, maybe we ought to clean up," he said suddenly.

"Are you in a hurry?" She pointed to his full wineglass. "I thought you wanted wine."

"I'm not feeling too well." He couldn't explain to her the bridge he'd just jumped off.

"It's come upon you rather quickly." She reached over to feel his forehead, and Garrison jumped at her cool touch. "You don't feel hot."

"I don't know what it is." He got up from the table hurriedly so she wouldn't touch him anymore.

"Maybe I kept you in the sun too long." She got up, following him to where he hovered at the kitchen sink. "I'm sorry, Garrison. Farm work is tough when you're not used to it. You're so fair-skinned, and that blond hair of yours probably catches sun rays bigtime. I hope I didn't make you ill."

He stared at her pretty lips as she spoke. How could he ever explain to her that she truly was the problem in his life? A problem which had brought him to a crisis he hadn't been prepared to face?

But the die was cast. There was no going back.

She placed one of her cool palms against his cheek. "Can I get you a cool glass of water? Would that help?"

He gulped. Dixie had no idea what a vision she was in her white scoop-necked eyelet blouse and candy pink shorts that hugged her adorable bottom. Looking at her was far more refreshing to his hungry eyes than a glass of water could ever be. "No, thank you," he croaked.

"Do you want me to take you home?" She smiled,

a bit teasingly. "You've paid me back in full, especially with this wonderful meal you helped prepare."

He could hardly breathe with her touching him. He took her hand, removing it from his cheek and slowly moved it to her side. She looked at him in concern. "I'm sorry you don't feel well. Do you want to go upstairs and lie down?"

That was the last thing he needed, to lie in Dixie's bed surrounded by her scent in a room that so clearly held everything she loved. "I can't. At the risk of being a bad guest, I'd better go." His phone call and financial situation weighed heavily on him.

"You're not a bad guest." Her blue eyes sparkled at him. "You'll miss what I wanted to show you, but you can see my bicycle built for two another time. If you'd like," she said shyly, obviously trying to let him know that he was welcome to return another day if he wanted to.

His heart thundered in his chest. Somehow he wasn't the least bit disappointed. Scared, maybe. Dixie's vehicular contraptions were part of her charm—he was in danger from both. "That's what you wanted me in one piece for?"

"Oh, yes." She nodded. "I need someone to ride it with me. My grandparents used to love to ride through the fields on it. Grandpa gave it to me when I moved here," she said with an innocence he found disarming, "and it's just been waiting."

"Waiting?"

"For the right man, maybe."

Her sweet smile sneaked into his soul. He'd seen his name in the heart she'd drawn, and now he knew what that meant. For some unfathomable reason, Dixie Adams thought he was her right man. She'd saved something precious, the odd two-seated family bike for her prince. She would *never* be a Ferrari kind of girl.

He stared into her eyes, tempted by goodness for the first time in his life.

Chapter Fifteen

Garrison backed away from Dixie slowly, heading toward the front door. "Dixie, I've got to go."

"Okay," she said softly. "Stay, Rascal." Picking up her fanny pack, she went out the door Garrison held open for her. Without a word, they got on her motorbike. It started competently, and they were off, leaving the doll's house and all its temptations behind.

Garrison breathed a sigh of relief under his helmet. It had been a very narrow miss. He had to get back to his world so that he could think clearly. Everything was about to cave in on him, and Dixie's allure was clouding the picture.

His mind raced with disjointed thoughts, so that when she pulled up at his house, he was surprised. Hopping off the bike, he put the helmet away. "Thanks for the ride. Both of them."

"No problem." Her eyes watched him with uncertainty.

"I had a good time." Garrison couldn't think of anything else to say in this awkward moment. He could see the hope written on Dixie's countenance.

"I did, too." She turned the motorcycle around.

"Hope you get your Ferrari taken care of." But she didn't mention anything more about him getting a job with Ned, which had been a patently ridiculous suggestion, anyway. What would he be doing driving a taxi? His well-heeled buddies would laugh themselves into oxygen debt.

Her face turned toward the road. She was about to leave him behind. "Wait, Dixie," Garrison suddenly called. He strode to her side, gently unstrapping her helmet and removing it. Then he kissed her, long and hungrily. He kissed those sassy lips as if he never would again, hanging on to each second of the rich sensation. Her lips were soft and pliable under his, and Garrison groaned inside. The woman had lures that hooked into the most irretrievable places in his soul.

Regretfully he ended the kiss, putting her helmet back on with hands that were glad for something to do. She didn't move, her posture tense with unanswered questions.

He had no answers to give her. "Good night," he murmured.

"Good night." She glanced at him one last time before zooming off into the night. He stared after her until he could no longer hear the engine, then turned toward the house.

Parker's Mercedes was parked in front. He went up to it, peeking inside curiously. *What a machine,* he thought with envy. Oozing expense and luxury and made for a man who knew what he wanted out of life. Garrison ran one longing palm over the hood and reluctantly went inside the house.

He spied keys lying on the entry hall table as if they'd been left there in a hurry. Stepping closer, he saw the Mercedes emblem. His blood ran cold in his veins as he glanced around for the owner. The house was quiet. Parker and Noreen were probably upstairs watching TV with Meg, as they'd done once before. The aunts weren't in residence. Everything was still, and as the keys sent out their undeniable call to him, Garrison thought about his poor, broken-down Ferrari he couldn't afford to have repaired. How he'd love to have wheels that worked, and worked well!

Just once, he wanted to drive a car like that one out front. Just once...

MEG HAD FALLEN ASLEEP in Noreen's arms. She'd been rubbing the child's back while Noreen lay propped against Parker's chest, and after one cartoon, Meg had snoozed off. Nearby, Noreen could hear the grasshopper jumping around in its pail, which Meg had insisted on bringing upstairs. The room was dim, lit only by the TV. With Parker's arms around her, Noreen felt as if the three of them were in a cocoon, cozy and together.

She wondered if it could last. "If you don't mind, I'd like to pick Meg up a pair of jeans and boots," she said. Leaning back so that her head tucked up under his neck, she sighed. "The next time you two come out here, I'll take her shopping, if that's okay."

"Fine by me, if I can come. Shopping for clothes is such an ordeal for Meg and me that we haven't enjoyed it very much. I tend to let her grandmother do the buying."

Hence the adorable, fluffy church dresses. Noreen closed her eyes. *If she was my daughter, I'd want to dress her up like a doll, too.* "Will her grandmother be shocked the first time Meg shows up in jeans?"

He chuckled. "Lavinia's parents are far more easy-going than Lavinia ever dreamed of being. They're just honest and kind. They'll be happy if Meg has someone else who treats her like she's special."

"She is."

"Well, I know that, and they know that, but it's been a real source of heartache to them that—"

He broke off but Noreen heard the unspoken words. They were disappointed in their daughter's choice to leave her family behind. Noreen swallowed, realizing she'd stepped in painful territory. "Parker, I don't want to interfere if—"

"You're not." He ran smooth palms along her arms in a comforting manner. "There was no marriage discussion to be had. I called her while you napped."

"None?" Noreen waited, agonized, for him to remove the doubt that had been plaguing her all day.

"None. It's been too long, and I know Lavinia too well. She'll be off again soon." He sighed heavily. "There's nothing here for her. Dallas is too small and dull."

"Dull!" She'd had a most exciting—and discomfiting—time when she'd gone into Dallas for the ball. "Dull would define this farm, I suppose."

"I don't think so." He nipped light kisses along her neck. "When I took your relatives home tonight, I took some extra time just to drive around on the land I bought, back of their houses. I still think you ought to accept my wedding gift."

"I can't." She smiled, but it was bittersweet. "Parker, it's too much. I could never work it all by myself. But I did notice you were gone a long time."

"Miss me, did you?"

"Mmm."

He kissed her neck for that answer. "Well, what if I developed part of it? Built some small Mom and Pop type shops, with maybe an old-fashioned eatery for the tourists?"

Her scalp prickled uncomfortably as a nervous tingle swept over her. "That isn't as bad as a movieplex, I suppose."

"No." He hugged her to him. "It would bring some commerce to the area, but not make the landscape ugly and overrun."

Her heart sank as she realized there wouldn't be another farming family who moved into the Widow Martin's house. The open land she was used to seeing would eventually present a different view. Yet, she was lucky that Parker had bought it instead of Jefferson Crower.

"Did you hear something?" She sat up suddenly.

"I...don't think so. I wasn't listening, frankly." He was feeling. The woman felt so good he could stay here forever holding her. One day, he hoped she'd let him.

"I'm positive I heard something outside!"

"Maybe it's Garrison."

"Oh." She relaxed back into his arms. "Of course." A moment later, footsteps up the stairs confirmed Parker's guess. They heard the sound of a door closing, signaling that Garrison had gone into his bedroom.

"He didn't stay out as late as I thought he would."

Parker didn't care. In spite of the benefit of the doubt Noreen gave her stepbrother, the man worried Parker. He had some kind of a grudge he directed at Noreen, and it bothered Parker. But saying so to Noreen would put him in her bad graces, so he kept his mouth shut. Gently disentangling himself, he sat up. "I've got to get my little princess home. Tomorrow's a work day."

Monday. Noreen hadn't given the day much thought. She'd been content to stay in this room with Parker and Meg, and hadn't felt the need to leave for a long time.

But the magical weekend was over. She rose reluctantly, watching as Parker scooped his daughter up into his arms. *He's such a good father.*

Following him downstairs, she noticed how still the house was. Quiet. In the summer, more night sounds usually filtered in, the sound of birds nesting and breezes blowing. She had the uncanny feeling that something wasn't quite right. *I'm just disappointed Parker is leaving. It's all so new it's got me jittery.*

She walked with him to his car, achingly aware of how much she was going to miss him. He'd get busy with his work week, she'd be busy with hers, and life would go on. Without him.

Suddenly her tennis shoe shot out from underneath her. She caught her balance, grabbing out in the darkness toward the car to steady herself.

"Are you all right?" Parker swiveled, reaching out to steady her with one hand.

"Yes. I'm usually not so clumsy." What if Parker had stepped on whatever she had and lost his footing with Meg in his arms? She couldn't imagine what had made the ground so slick! He bent to put Meg inside the car, and suddenly Noreen realized what was off about the night.

The aroma of pumpkin carried to her, thick on the air. Stooping, she squinted at the place where she'd slipped. The inside car lights weren't much help. "Can you turn on your headlights?"

"Sure." He reached to the dash to flip them on. "What are you looking at?"

"Someone threw a pumpkin at your tire," she told him. "Look." With the extra light, they could see pumpkin remains all over the tire. Some seeds and stringy pumpkin strands stuck to Noreen's heel. "That's what I slipped on."

"They got this tire, too." He walked around the car, examining it in the darkness. "I need a flashlight to see better, but I'd say they got all four."

"I wonder who would do such a thing?" Noreen stood. "I'm going to the field, in case the vandals are still out there."

"You're not going without me." He glanced inside the car where Meg lay across the back seat, sound asleep. Scooping her back up, Parker followed Noreen from the front yard to the north-lying field.

He heard her cry out. The sound jarred him into running as fast as he could. "What happened?" he called. His mind imagined all kinds of things. Maybe she'd stepped on a snake. Maybe someone had thrown a pumpkin at her.

He halted at her side, glancing at her face immediately. Her hands were pressed to her mouth. Turning to see what had her riveted, Parker's jaw dropped in disbelief. As far as he could see into the darkness, no more green balls dotted the ground.

The whole pumpkin field appeared destroyed.

SHOCKED, Noreen walked into the field, or maybe it was more of a desperate search for the extent of the damage. Perhaps only a few feet of pumpkins had been ruined. Her heart was in her throat, her dreams in pieces at her feet. "Oh, no," she murmured. She couldn't believe her eyes. Nowhere could she find a single whole pumpkin. Something had happened, something terrible, and all she could think of was that Parker had been gone awhile tonight and now his tires were covered in pumpkin mush.

It was insane, of course. Parker would never hurt her. He would never destroy her crop. It didn't matter that he was a real estate tycoon, because he had proved he wasn't dating her so that he could be in the right place at the right time should she ever decide to sell. Now she'd lost her one crop that represented profit, but Noreen still knew Parker wasn't capable of sabotaging her.

But she desperately wished her mind hadn't briefly wondered if he could have.

PARKER SAW the numb disbelief on Noreen's face. He ached to help her, but there was nothing he could do. Surely she had insurance to cover the damage, but that wouldn't make her feel better now. All her hard work was gone, and money couldn't replace that. He stood silent with his child in his arms, feeling useless. Who would want to do this to Noreen?

Garrison blew into his mind. Garrison might stand to benefit from his sister's bad fortune. He'd come home earlier than expected, after calling to say he'd be in late. Oh, that had been convenient. Everyone had been so glad to have him gone that they'd only marveled at his sudden manners.

He bit the inside of his jaw as he watched Noreen stand like a sleepwalker among her ruined plants. She wasn't going to want to believe Garrison would do such a thing. She believed in him. The fact was, this might be the crowning blow to her farm. If she sold, Garrison would get the money he so badly wanted— even more now that his prized Ferrari wasn't going to run again without an infusion of cash to pay the repair bill.

He worried how much it would hurt her when she finally realized who was behind this plot.

TOGETHER they walked inside the house. Noreen found herself shaking, her stomach muscles tight with nerves. Her grandmother and aunts were used to walking home together across the length of field for exercise. What if Parker hadn't driven them home tonight? What if they'd come upon the vandals?

Parker had said he'd driven around awhile after he'd taken Hattie, Priscilla and Charlene home. Noreen swallowed hard. "Guess I should call the police," she murmured.

"I'll do it."

He crossed to the phone, dialed the number swiftly and began relating the happenings to someone on the other end. Noreen sank into a chair. No, Parker wasn't guilty, but her trust in him wasn't quite solid yet. And she was shaken! When he hung up, Noreen looked at him with despair in her heart.

"I think I'll call my grandmother and Aunt Hattie and Aunt Charlene to make sure they're all right." She hesitated. "Maybe I shouldn't. It just might scare them."

"I'll go check on them." Parker rose.

"No!"

He was startled by her vehement opposition. "Why not?"

"Someone used your car for target practice. The police might want to see."

Nodding, he leaned against the wall, his arms crossed. "You're right. Good thinking."

Her muscles relaxed. They were in this together. He was on her side. "You know," she said quietly, "it would appear to me that someone either enjoyed vandalizing you, or they were trying to frame you."

"Frame me?" He looked at her, his brows drawn in a frown.

"Throw suspicion on you. Make it look like you drove through my pumpkin fields."

His mouth opened slightly in surprise. "Why would I do that?"

"I don't know. But I bet the police ask you where you went tonight."

He pushed off the wall. "I…hadn't thought of that."

"I know." She looked at him sadly. "I think they will."

Pacing the kitchen, he shook his head. "The only person that I figured they'd suspect was Garrison."

"Garrison?" Now she was confused. "My brother wouldn't do that."

"Wouldn't he?" Parker turned to look at her, his expression curious.

"No, he wouldn't!" She jumped to her feet. "Parker, he doesn't even have a running vehicle!"

"No, but my car keys were lying on the hall table. I tossed them there when I carried Meg upstairs. She wanted up in my arms, and I set them down and picked her up."

She was stunned. "You really think he might have stolen your car to take a joyride through my crops?"

He rubbed his forehead. "I don't know what to think. Who else would do it? Not your aunts and grandmother. That leaves Garrison or plain, old hoodlums." Considering that for a moment, he said, "I remember trick-or-treating when I was a kid. Some kids liked to steal jack-o'-lanterns off porches and either kick them in or throw them and watch them bust. Punting pumpkins seemed pretty harmless then, but..." He shook his head. "Maybe it was hoodlums, and they couldn't resist bombing my car with them, too."

Her head drooped. "I think we would have heard such a commotion."

"Yeah. Whoever it was certainly was quiet."

Of course, Noreen had been lost in her own world with Meg and Parker. Sighing heavily, she leaned back in a chair. "Maybe I should go upstairs and ask Garrison if he noticed anything strange when he came home."

"That's a great idea."

He walked behind Noreen, but stayed at the foot of the stairs as she made her way up reluctantly. The whole situation didn't make a bit of sense! She was torn between crying over the loss of her possible bumper crop—the best she'd had in years—and anger over who would be so cruel. They had no idea what they'd stolen from her. She felt Parker's eyes on her as she gained the top of the stairs. For the second time she desperately wished her mind hadn't instantly wondered about his involvement. But it was obvious someone had wanted suspicion pointed at him or they wouldn't have bothered with his car.

She felt ill. Maybe Garrison had heard a strange noise as she had earlier, and they could come up with a possible theory. Of course, Garrison had come in after she'd heard the strange thumping noise. That realization made her feel even more ill, so she hurried to knock on his door.

There was no answer. She knocked again, harder, in case he was asleep. He might as well know they'd summoned the police, then he wouldn't be awakened by the sound of people in their home.

"Garrison!" she called through the door, not too loudly in case she woke Meg, whom Parker had put back in the guest bedroom. There was no sound from inside her stepbrother's room, so Noreen cautiously opened the door and scanned the bed.

He wasn't there, nor in the adjoining bathroom. Noreen's shoulders slumped as she went back to the top of the stairs and looked down to where Parker still waited.

"He's not here," she said dully.

Chapter Sixteen

"I was afraid of that," Parker replied.

"Why?" she demanded sharply, coming slowly down the stairs.

"He's the only one who stands to gain from you losing the crop." He shrugged. "He's certainly not emotionally involved in your success."

"I don't like what you're saying," she said hotly. "I know it looks bad, but Garrison wouldn't—"

The doorbell rang, its merry peal slicing across her words. Noreen stalked away from Parker to open the door. Two uniformed officers stood outside, identification in hand, but she knew both of them from high school.

"Hi, Cal. Hey, Bob." She stepped back to admit the big men, both football players from their glorious school years.

"Took a look at the mess outside with my flashlight, Noreen. Sorry it had to happen to ya." Bob eyed Parker. "Who've we got here?"

Parker immediately stiffened under the officer's critical eye. First of all, he'd seen how the men greeted Noreen, affectionately at the least, perhaps with interest at the most. Neither of them were married, and both of them were hulking, somewhat decent-looking men. Second, he didn't like the curiosity in Bob's eyes, which was directed at him. "I'm Parker Walden," he said, reaching out to shake Bob's hand nevertheless and then Cal's.

"Haven't seen you around here before," Cal commented.

"No. I'm no relation to Noreen."

He wanted to say *yet,* just so they'd get that silly ogle out of their eyes, but that would make Noreen uncomfortable, so he stuffed his male ego back into its cave and excused himself to go get a glass of water from the kitchen.

"This gonna set you back a bit, Noreen?" he heard Bob ask.

"More than a bit." She sighed, the sound rich with disappointment. "It was my profit crop."

"Well, heck. Let's get to tracking, Cal, and see what we can turn up."

Very little, Parker thought sourly. Those two appeared to have a lot of muscle and not much gray matter between them. He sighed, recognizing jealousy when it bit him. It wasn't personal, he reminded himself. The cops had to check him out, as they would anyone else who was a stranger in Noreen's home. He had simply been put off by their appreciative glances toward Noreen, and no doubt, he'd feel much better when they directed their cop curiosity toward Garrison, as well.

"Know anybody who might do this, Noreen?" Cal asked.

Parker heard the front door open and then her answer.

"No. I still can't believe it's happened," she said.

Parker frowned in surprise. Was she going to say nothing about Garrison coming in and then leaving without a word—especially after his big show of calling everyone to let them know he'd be staying out late? All the women had appeared astounded by his development of courtesy.

"Anybody else on the property tonight?"

She hesitated. Parker couldn't stand it any longer. He went to stand in the foyer beside Noreen, and stared the police down.

"My brother was here for a little while," she murmured. "And my grandmother and aunts for dinner, but Parker drove them home."

Instantly she seemed to realize what she'd said. Her eyes widened in an "oops" expression. The officers' gazes trained on Parker in tandem wariness. He didn't move a muscle.

"Well, I wouldn't put any money on Garrison doing it," Bob said mildly, turning to head out onto the porch with his lug of a companion.

"Nah," Cal agreed, guffawing loudly. "He's always been a bit light in his Eye-talian loafers."

"And lazy as an old hound." Bob headed toward the cruiser. "I'll get the other flashlight."

Noreen slowly turned to meet Parker's furious gaze. "I'm sorry," she said. "I know what you're thinking. But I didn't mean—"

"You didn't mean to focus them on me any more than they already are, but you didn't mention that your brother had conveniently arrived and departed during the pumpkin-smashing fun!" He was furious with Noreen, for the first time realizing that her loyalty was so deep for her good-for-nothing brother that she might actually hang Parker out to dry. Anger ran through him like fire.

"I have to give him the benefit of the doubt!"

"You've told me that before. But you also assured me I'd get it, too!"

"You do! And you are!" she cried. "I don't think you did it, Parker!"

"But you wondered." He stared into her eyes. "Deny it."

She backed away. "I'm ashamed to say that…it briefly crossed my mind. But I know you wouldn't!"

"No, I wouldn't," he ground out, his voice rough. "One might suspect that you did it yourself to get insurance money. Be a lot easier than waiting out the vagaries of Mother Nature."

She gasped, her hand flying to her throat. "How dare you!"

"How dare you?" He strode to the kitchen, then came back out again. "I assume I'm as free to leave as Garrison, because I sure as hell want to."

"Oh, Parker." Noreen's shoulders drooped. "Please. I can't bear it if you do. Especially angry. I…need you." She slowly looked up to meet his gaze, distraught.

He rubbed the bridge of his nose. "Do you mean you need a fall guy?"

"No. I know Garrison didn't do it, but I know you didn't, either." She turned away to look out the door. In the distance, they could hear Bob and Cal calling to one another.

Parker blew out a disgusted breath. "Do you think those two would be capable of finding their way out of their own backyards without maps?"

"Why do you ask that?"

"Well, you can't deny they're not exactly going to set a record for intelligence."

Her frown line deepened. "Are you stereotyping them, Parker? Because they're not city cops?"

He sensed deep water. "No. I just meant that they don't seem that sharp. Polished."

"I wasn't as polished as the other women at the charity ball," she shot back. "I'm a farmer from Rockwall, Texas. Would that have made me less than your former companions? After all, I've lived here most of my life, among people like Bob and Cal and Ned Adams who are as nice as the day is long and who know what really matters in life."

She turned her face away. His jaw dropped. "I think I've got a feel for what really matters in life."

"Do you?" She didn't look at him. "So why can't you understand that my brother is important to me, because he mattered to my father? I can't wash my hands of him, even if he is guilty, which I know he is not. And all that glitters is not gold, Parker. There are just as much riches in the soil, if you could see it as something other than a financial venture." She shrugged. "Maybe living in the city makes a person sophisticated but not necessarily wiser."

"Hey." He reached out to gently tug her arm to pull her toward him. "I'm sorry I mouthed off about your friends. I didn't mean it as a personal attack on you. My nature is to want the best people to tackle the jobs that need to be done."

"So give them a chance," she stated, not melting against him as she usually did. "They pick on Garrison, but only because he always turned his nose up at them in school. They weren't good enough for him."

Her unyielding posture told him that he'd hurt her feelings. She was good enough for him—he'd never once considered her as anything less than a dream—but he could see how she would relate his remark about Cal and Bob to herself. Parker relaxed his grip on her a little, understanding that he'd crossed a line. Plus she was upset over her crop, and he shouldn't have jumped in with his opinion. She'd said before that she didn't need to be rescued, and obviously, she was capable of handling this disaster. Parker exhaled tensely and told himself to wait this situation out.

He hoped when it was over that he was still welcome at Cinderella Acres. And he wondered, more than idly, where Noreen's wicked stepbrother was hiding.

GARRISON HEARD the growl before he had a chance to climb up the veranda post that led to Dixie's window. It was too late to retreat. "Aargh!" he cried out, as warning teeth sank into his trousers. "Dixie!" he hollered. "Dixie!"

Her window raised. "Who's down there?"

Garrison shook Rascal off his pants and jumped up on the veranda post, wrapping his legs around it. "It's Garrison! Make Rascal—ow!"

He tried to scale farther, but the dog had fastened itself to the cuff of his trousers and was tugging with all his might.

The door flew open, and Dixie ran out. "Rascal! No!" She clapped her hands, and the dog let go, albeit reluctantly.

"I gave you ice out of my glass, you traitor!" Garrison couldn't believe the dog had been so determined to take a chunk out of him. "You've torn my pants!"

From the light flooding out the front door, he could see Rascal's smug doggy expression. Garrison sighed, decided the cuff could be replaced somehow and turned to look at Dixie.

The woman dressed was one thing; in a lacy sleep top and bottom, she looked even better. He felt his breath tighten in his chest.

"Are you all right, Garrison?" she asked. "Rascal! I know you were doing your job, but must you do it so thoroughly?" Giving the dog a pat, which earned Garrison another satisfied smirk from the beast, she glared at the trespasser. "What are you doing here, anyway?"

"I had to talk to you." It wasn't the world's best answer, but it was the truth.

"And I guess your phone line was out..."

"No." He shook his head. "It had to be face-to-face."

She paused, considering that. "How did you get here?"

"Do I have to tell you?"

"I think I'd better know now if you're expecting a ride home. I'm sure not dressed for it." Her lips pressed into a frown. Obviously she wasn't pleased about being dragged out of bed, and he couldn't blame her.

"Your bicycle built for two gave me an idea. I got my old bike I rode in high school out of the garage." He let his gaze travel over her face. The effort had been more than worth it.

"So you rode over here to talk to me?" Her voice held surprise.

"And I'm riding back home. You don't have to chauffeur me."

"I can't believe it. Garrison, what has gotten into you?"

"I'm not sure." He was almost as perplexed as she was.

"Well, what's so important that you had to see me at this hour?"

He scratched his neck, trying to get the courage up to tell her. "I've never met anyone like you before."

"I could say the same thing."

His name might have been encircled in her heart, but she wasn't going to throw herself at him. That was okay. He was willing to exert himself for a change. "Dixie, I don't think I'm ever going to be the same now that I've met you."

She pursed her lips, a gesture he found terribly sexy. "Is that good?"

"It may be the best thing that ever happened to me." He took a deep breath. "You rattle my cage, but I think I needed rattling real bad. I've been stuck inside my own head, and for the first time, I see that my life is pretty shallow."

She crossed her arms. "Garrison, I'm not a miracle worker. You have to change yourself."

He nodded. "I realize that. I don't know where we go from here. All I want you to know is that I shouldn't have run out on you earlier. I got nervous. You keep me turned pretty much inside out, and I think I knew where my heart was going but I had to take a minute to realign my mind." He cleared his throat, feeling the burn of dryness from his anxiety. "I'm going to change a lot more to get to the point where I deserve you, Dixie."

"Oh...I have to say I'm...speechless."

Her eyes were wide as she stared at him. Clearly,

she was astounded. He was, too. Two days ago, all he cared about was fast cars and beautiful women. Nobody would have dared suggest to him that he might fall for this spunky lady—or that he'd be willing to sell his Ferrari to get the money to take her out. "I know it will take a while for you to see that I'm sincere, but I'm willing to wait, if you think you can give me a probationary period."

"I just don't know what to say."

He reached out to touch her fingertips, and this time Rascal didn't growl from his watchful sitting position. "Say six months," he said huskily. "If I haven't measured up at any time in the next six months, you can simply say 'Deal's off.'"

"No time off for good behavior?" she asked, mock sternly.

"No. No cutting corners, no shirking."

After a moment, she slowly moved her hand into his, shaking it once. "It's a deal."

"You won't regret it." He lifted her fingertips to his lips, kissing them. Then he released her and stepped back. "I've got to start pedaling. By the time my six months is up, I'll be in excellent physical condition."

"When will your car be fixed?"

"I don't know. I'm going to sell it. Then maybe you'll help me pick out a practical vehicle." He grinned at her, feeling proud of himself for the first time in his life. "I wouldn't know one kind of truck from the other, and I have a funny feeling that one day we're going to need a hauling truck."

"Oh, Garrison," she breathed. "Maybe you're ill. Maybe this is just a dream, and tomorrow I'll wake up and realize you weren't here at all."

He reached up and broke a large twig off the tree his bike leaned against. On bended knee, he drew a big heart in the loamy dirt between them with the stick. Inside it he spelled *Dixie*.

"There," he said, looking up at her, "you can see that from your window in the morning. Then you'll know it wasn't a dream."

She clasped her hands together, smiling. "Okay."

"Of course, I suppose I have no guarantees that I won't wake up and find out I don't have a six-month probation period with you."

"You'll have really sore muscles in the morning," she said with that sassy smile he loved. "That'll let you know you weren't dreaming. But hang on." She went running up the porch steps, slamming the door behind her. The bedroom window raised, and a second later something white floated down, paper airplane style, to land at his feet. He picked it up and flattened out the creases. It was the note she'd drawn the heart on, with his name inside.

"That's my loan document. My heart for up to six months, renewable at that time if both parties agree."

He kissed the paper and waved it at her before pedaling off on his bike. It was the best deal he'd ever made, and tomorrow, he was going to call Ned Adams and see if he was willing to take on an apprentice. After all, he had to have a job, and he might as well start greasing the wheels where Grandpa was concerned.

Because one day, he intended to ask Ned Adams a more serious question: Dixie's hand in marriage was his final goal. The thought of living here with her, helping her with her farm, maybe adding a limousine to Ned's taxi business, made his heart soar as he pedaled off into the darkness.

Rascal chased his bike all the way to the end of the lane, playfully barking at the tires. He had six months to convince Rascal, too. That could be solved with ice, but Dixie wouldn't be so easy to win over.

For once in his life he looked forward to hard work.

BOB AND CAL had departed to the field, so Noreen and Parker sat at the kitchen table, keeping a wary vigil. Parker sensed the worry Noreen was trying to hide.

He knew Garrison was on her mind, even if she wouldn't admit it for the world. Parker tried to look at the situation from a logical standpoint. Even Garrison wasn't stupid enough to do something so obvious to sabotage his stepsister, although the pumpkin remains on the Mercedes's tires did bother him. He thought Garrison had paid so little attention to his presence in Noreen's life that it was unlikely he would have been driven to frame him.

He drummed his fingers on the table and considered the alternative: merely teenagers out for a prank. Maybe that was all it was.

Noreen got up from the table and paced the kitchen. "They won't find anything. Not tonight. It's too dark."

Parker thought she was probably right but decided to try to reassure her instead. "You've explained to me that they're some of Rockwall's finest. Your faith has always kept you in good stead."

"Yes." She rubbed her hands over her arms. "Maybe I'm being unrealistic. I don't think I can bear finding out that someone I know ruined my field."

At least he was lumped in with Garrison, Parker thought, and that was a good sign. She believed very little ill of her stepbrother. "Noreen, sit down and try to relax. Please."

"I can't seem to." She peered out the window over the sink, then whirled to face him. "Where could Garrison be? He has no car, but he was here and then he was gone!"

"Don't let doubt start eating at you now." Parker got up to stand behind her, rubbing her shoulders.

"I'm trying not to." But her body was tense.

Suddenly there was a huge ruckus outside. It sounded like men's laughter, and something crashing, as well as a loud cry.

Noreen jumped. "What in heaven's name was that?"

GARRISON WAS RIDING on winged wheels. Dixie Adams hadn't refused his suit out-of-hand! Tomorrow he was going to ride over to talk to Ned and see what he could get lined up.

First, maybe he'd better talk to his sister and tell her he wasn't selling his share of the farm. He'd put her through enough agony, and he wasn't proud of his behavior. Then he needed to talk to the car repair shop and find out just what was wrong with the Ferrari. Selling it should be a breeze. From there, he'd start looking for appropriate vehicles for a family man.

So intent was he on his dreams that he didn't see the two burly shadows jump to waylay his bike as he rode up the darkened lane toward the porch. They had him before he even hit the ground. "Aiy-ay!" he screamed. "Help!"

"Ah, heck. It's just Garrison." One set of hands picked him up none too gently off the ground and dusted him off. Another hand whacked him on the back before setting his bike back up. "Hush, Garrison. It's just Bob."

"And Cal. Sheesh, you scream like a woman."

"What in the name of Sam do you two think you're doing?" Garrison demanded, jerking his bike out of Cal's hands and glaring at his old schoolmates' faces. His elbow hurt from jamming into a thickly muscled thigh, and they'd nearly scared half a year off him by blowing up his fantasies about his new life. "You could have hurt me, you baboons!"

He heard chuckles. "Hey, where's your Lamborghini?" Bob asked.

"It's a Ferrari," he gritted out. "Where's your brains?"

"Ah, still the same old Garrison. Sensitive, skinny thing," Cal said. "Since when did you start taking up night cycling?"

"I haven't. My car's in the shop." Garrison glared at them, thoroughly incensed. "Since you're not on official business, and since I don't feel like standing around talking to two big-headed idiots, you'll have to excuse me." He started to pull the bike up on the porch.

"Hang on just a sec more, buddy." Cal popped his knuckles. "What do you know about that city boy hanging around your sister?"

"Not much, except that she seems to fancy him better than either of you. Too bad, huh?"

"Yeah, wouldn't want to mix our gene pool with yours." Cal grinned.

"Might turn out some sissies," Bob agreed. "Runts."

"Might turn out more grunting jocks with sub-zero IQ's, too," Garrison pointed out. "But at least they'd be pretty. What's your problem with Parker, anyway?"

"Reckon he likes her," Bob commented.

"Tough for you." Garrison shrugged. "Do I have to stand here and listen to your wishful thinking? I'm sorry about Noreen, but she's her own woman, and obviously, thick-skulled he-men aren't her idea of dream date material. Can't help you further, guys." He wanted to pop off something about it would take a shrink and maybe new faces for the kind of help they needed, but they looked so serious suddenly that he became fully aware that he was stranded between them.

"Garrison, cool your mouth for a minute and tell us what you know about Parker Walden." Cal looked so intent that Garrison swallowed.

"Is something wrong? Did something happen to Noreen?" His blood chilled just thinking about it. Tweedle Dee and Tweedle Dum had never paid him a social call before.

"Your pumpkin patch got vandalized," Bob said simply. "Someone drove a car through the field and smashed all the crop, as far as we can tell. Get a better look when the sun comes up, but right now, I'd say you're out of the pumpkin business."

"Oh, no!" Garrison jerked his head to look toward the north, but he couldn't see very far in the dark. "Why would—does Noreen know?"

"Yeah."

Oh, she had to be devastated. And probably crying.

Garrison was glad Parker was with his sister to comfort her. "I'd better get inside."

"Where've you been, anyway, Garrison?"

"I've been...hey, I sure as hell didn't do it! My car's in the shop!" He was incensed. He'd considered a lot of underhanded things in his life, but ruining a good crop wasn't one of them. Usually too much rain, lack of it, bugs or fungus was enough to keep a field from seeing its potential. He wouldn't have had to sink to sabotage.

"Maybe you drove someone else's car," Cal suggested. "Like that one." He pointed toward Parker's Mercedes.

"I don't think so. I haven't been pedaling this stupid bike for my health!" Garrison snapped. "And I'm not a car thief!"

"So why have you been cycling?" Bob asked reasonably. "It's a little too economical for your blood."

"Not that it's any of you sorry loser's business, but I was seeing a girl," he said between gritted teeth.

"On a bike! Garrison Cartwright romancing on a old bicycle!" Cal laughed heartily.

"She must be some slim pickings to let you come around on a bike," Bob agreed. "Bottom of the barrel for sure."

"I was over to see Dixie Adams, for your information, if you must know in your official capacity." Garrison was hopping mad about being snatched off his bike like some common criminal and now being the object of their belittlement.

"Dixie Adams?" they repeated in unison.

"That ain't no bottom of the barrel," Bob said in wonder.

"You're lying like a rug, Garrison," Cal stated.

"I've asked Dixie out three times and she told me she wasn't ready to date anyone. Said she was too busy with her farm."

He put his bike up on the porch where nobody could trip over it. "Ah, well. Best man wins and all that. Good night." He went inside and slammed the door.

He'd never stood up to those guys before. His chest puffed a bit with pride. All that smart-mouth stuff and attitude he'd picked up from Dixie, and it felt great not letting those doorknob-headed creeps walk all over him. Well, they weren't all that bad, but they sure had rode him rough in high school.

He felt like a million bucks knowing that Dixie had picked him. It was the sweetest feeling he'd ever known.

Winning her would be the highlight of his whole life.

PARKER WOULDN'T let Noreen run out to intervene, though she could clearly see from the window that Cal and Bob were deviling her stepbrother.

"I thought you said they were good officers," Parker stated. "So let them do their job."

"But they're obviously picking on him!" She shook off his arm. "It's left over from high school stuff. You wouldn't understand!"

"I understand you're rushing in to protect him once again." He put his arm around her. "You don't do either of you a favor by refusing to admit that he's not helpless, Noreen. He's a grown man. Let him get out of his own predicament for a change."

She couldn't believe he could be so callous. "You

don't like my brother. You hope they take him in for questioning!''

"You said you didn't think he was guilty, and I think you're probably right. But they've got to do their job, honey.''

Without thinking, she pulled away from him, crossing her arms in a defensive stance. "Parker, I realize you don't understand our lives. You haven't known us, known how hard it was losing both of our parents. Maybe I haven't always done the right thing for Garrison, but I've sure tried.'' She took a deep breath. "All I know is, you had just as much opportunity as Garrison to do it, just as much motive, but you're not the one the cops are picking on.''

"You said it was leftover rivalry.''

"Yes,'' she said sadly. "But that doesn't change the fact that they aren't questioning you. They're questioning him. And I've got to be with him, whether you understand that or not.'' She stared at him, her eyes bright with tears. "I'm all Garrison's got. If Bob and Cal say you can leave, I think you ought to go back to Dallas.'' She took a shaky breath. "I'm sorry.''

"Not nearly as sorry as I am.'' He was building up a little righteous anger of his own. "You've decided it has to be either me or Garrison in your life, but Noreen, it's time for you to cut the proverbial apron strings. He'll never grow up being smothered.''

"I'm not going to stand here and argue with you.'' She turned toward the door. "My father would want me to look out for him. It's something I have to do. Quite frankly, he needs me...and you do not.'' She met his gaze with determination of her own. "I'm going to stick by him.''

Chapter Seventeen

The door handle turned under her fingers, even as she and Parker stared at each other in a frozen moment of battling emotions. Noreen pulled back as the door opened. Garrison walked inside the foyer wearing a satisfied grin on his face.

"Are you all right?" Noreen demanded.

Her stepbrother glanced at her. "Sure. Why wouldn't I be? Hey, Parker. We've got a hose near the rose bushes if you want to clean off your car." He developed a really huge smirk when Cal and Bob followed him into the foyer. "If these fine officers of the peace give you their permission to, of course."

Cal and Bob shot him disgruntled glances before training their gazes on Parker.

"Well," Bob said, "Mr. Walden won't have time right away to wash his car. We'd like to take you down to the police station for questioning, sir."

"Questioning?" Noreen was astonished. "Bob! Do you have to?"

"I'm afraid we'd be remiss if we didn't cover all aspects of this investigation," Bob said sincerely. "You said yourself he left the property for a while."

Noreen glanced at Parker. Their eyes locked together in a moment of painful intensity. Garrison hadn't been at the premises either, but she couldn't bring herself to say that. Apparently Bob and Cal had questioned him just a moment ago, finding themselves satisfied with his alibi.

Parker had no alibi.

"He wasn't gone that long!" Distraught, she said, "You know it would take at least thirty minutes to destroy a field that size!"

"I apologize, Noreen. But we have to do our job." Cal looked truly regretful. "As his car has evidence on it, and he did leave the property for what you estimated was longer than twenty minutes, we have to take his statement."

Her gaze sank to the floor. She had wanted to go rushing out to Garrison's defense, but Parker wouldn't let her. He'd been right. Garrison had done just fine by himself, but she'd managed to place Parker in a truly awkward position.

"Let's get this over with." Parker moved toward the door. "Noreen, will you keep an eye on Meg until I get back?"

"Oh, of course!" She felt so guilty she would have agreed to anything, but watching Meg wasn't a hardship at all. "Parker, I'm so sorry!"

He barely looked at her as he left with Bob and Cal. He didn't say anything, either.

She had just told him to go back to Dallas. A sinking feeling filled her. No doubt he would return to Dallas when this ordeal was over—and be glad to leave her and Cinderella Acres behind.

"MAN ALIVE!" Garrison watched with Noreen as Parker got into the squad car. It drove away, without

Parker ever looking out at them. "Hope his legal counsel doesn't mind being awakened in the night, because Parker sure looks mad enough to breathe flames. Can't say that I blame him, though."

He turned to Noreen, but she was too upset to say anything. She couldn't believe this whole incident was really happening.

"Come inside, Noreen," Garrison said quietly, propelling her toward the kitchen. "Let me fix you a glass of tea. Or would you rather have something stronger?"

"No, that would make me tired. I'd rather have the tea." She shook her head, dazed by the events. "I'm going upstairs to check on Meg for a second, in case she awakened."

But the little girl was sound asleep, her hands tucked up under her chin. Noreen smoothed Meg's hair off her face, made sure the closet door was open a crack, the light on inside. Then she went back down to the kitchen to wait with her stepbrother.

"Will they give him a ride home when they're through talking to him?" she asked worriedly. "I'm not sure he'd call me to come get him."

"I don't know. They're probably not staffed well enough to return him. Why don't you think he'd call you?" Garrison put a glass on the table for each of them, and sank onto a straw-seated chair.

Noreen joined him, taking a sip of tea that did nothing to relax her. "I'd just finished telling him he ought to head back to Dallas, when Bob and Cal came in to take him to the station."

"What'd you do that for?" He looked at her curiously.

She wondered at this new Garrison, who was actually interested in her problems. He seemed so different these last couple of days. The change was almost...mystical. As if he were under a spell of sorts. She wrapped her hands around her glass and decided maybe he could handle the truth.

"We had been arguing about you." Her heart felt like it was breaking to have to say it.

"Me?" Garrison's astonishment was real. "What do I have to do with him going back to Dallas?"

"We don't see you quite the same way. I feel it's my responsibility to look after you...and Parker seems to think you should be looking after yourself. That I'm overcompensating for your mother passing away to the point that it's imposing on your life."

"Oh." He rubbed the back of his neck sheepishly. "Uh, Noreen, I know I've given you plenty of reasons to feel the way you do, but you don't have to take your responsibility as seriously anymore." He reached over to pat her wrist. "I hate that I was the cause of disagreement between you and Parker. Truthfully, I've been envious of him, but I wouldn't like to see you break up. Especially not over me."

She was stunned. "Garrison, can I ask you something?"

"Sure. Go ahead."

He reclined in his chair, looking more like the old, unhurried stepbrother. Maybe it was all an illusion, she thought, a mirage. Could he have been putting on an act? She didn't know. "You seem different lately. In the last few days, you've...I don't know what it is." He was as different as if he'd suddenly changed into an alien life-form. "What's gotten into you?"

"Well, Sis," he said with a cagey smile, "have you heard of the expression, love hurts?"

"Yes," she said, uncertain as to where he was going with that.

"I think that best applies to Dixie Adams," he said with a broad grin. "Meeting her was the single most painful experience in my life. True, pain-in-the-neck, got-me-by-the-seat-of-my-pants trauma." He couldn't contain his happiness, which shone from his eyes. "I guess you could say she is one of those life-altering events you hear about."

"Dixie Adams?" Noreen found it difficult to believe that Garrison would have anything to do with a woman he previously considered a country bumpkin. How could she have wrought such a startling change in her stepbrother? "I didn't think she was your type."

"Neither did I." He grinned. "But she changed my mind. And me." Leaning forward, he said earnestly, "I'm going to get a job."

Noreen raised her eyebrows. "A job?"

"For the first time in my life, I'm going to pay income tax," he said proudly.

"The government will be glad to hear that," she said drily, not certain if she should believe him.

"I don't know how I can help you with the pumpkins you lost, though. I know that was the profit crop."

She felt like she was caught in a whirling galaxy of amazement. "I thought you wanted to sell your part of Cinderella Acres."

His expression turned shamed. "I did. But not anymore." He reached out to touch her hand. "Noreen, I haven't been good to you. I've been spoiled and selfish, and you would have been smart to put me out years ago."

"I wouldn't," she said hurriedly.

"I knew that, and I abused your kindness. I wish I hadn't acted so badly," he said truthfully. "I've got a lot to make up to you for."

"I hardly know what to say, Garrison." She stared at her stepbrother, bewildered beyond comprehension at the change in him. "What's in the past is in the past," she finally said. "We'll go forward from here."

"I don't expect you to forgive me that easily."

"Oh, Garrison. You've had a tough row to hoe. We both have, and we've both made some mistakes." She smiled at him. "I'd rather forget about it all and start over. But feel free to bring Dixie around anytime. If she's the cause of your transformation, I'd like to get to know her better."

"Oh, she's great." Garrison sat straight, his smile big for a moment, before saying, "Probably as good for me as Parker is for you."

"Do you think so?" Noreen flushed just thinking about Parker. How she wished she hadn't spoken those angry words!

"I think now that I've reassured you that you don't have to look after me anymore, maybe you better go tell him you've got one less responsibility hanging around your neck." He leaned back in the chair again. "You might also tell him he was right."

She paused in the act of standing up. "Should I really say that?"

"Probably." He gave a casual wave. "A man likes to hear it once in a while. Soothes the ego."

"I'll take that…brotherly advice into consideration. I hope he'll see me, so I can tell him how sorry I am. He probably wishes he'd never met me."

"I doubt that seriously. But I do think you'd better go give him the same support you've always given me."

She hugged Garrison in a burst of unashamed pride. "I like the new you," she whispered.

"Surprisingly enough, so do I." He kissed her cheek, then pushed her away. "Go on. You leave him down there long enough and he may get the impression that you don't care about him."

"Okay." Hurriedly, she called her grandmother, Priscilla, to ask if she could drop Meg off over at her house.

"I'll watch my future niece," Garrison offered when she hung up the phone.

"I appreciate it, but Parker doesn't know about your metamorphosis," she said in a rush, so unsettled she didn't notice the sly hint Garrison had thrown in. "Anyway, you can help Grandmother and the aunts. Priscilla didn't want me to wake Meg, so they're all coming over to watch her. We shouldn't be long, but if Meg wakes up and is worried about her daddy being gone, show her the pail I put beside her bed. It'll make her happy to see her hoppergrass."

"Thanks for the hint. All of them are coming over?"

"Well, Grandma said Hattie would split like a boiled pea if she found out I'd asked only her to baby-sit, and she didn't dare leave Charlene out because then her feelings would be hurt." Noreen hurriedly swiped a hand through her hair. "You know how they are."

"I know. I used to resent that, but not anymore. Now I realize how lucky I've been."

She whirled to face him. "Garrison, go easy on

them with the new you, okay? I'm not sure they can stand the shock. I like it, but I've got to admit, the change is incredible." She waved and hurried out the door.

Inside, her heartbeat raced painfully. What if Parker didn't want to see her?

HATTIE WALKED into the house, accompanied by her two sisters. She sat down in an overstuffed chair in the living room, piercing Garrison with a gimlet eye as she pulled out her knitting. "So. What's got Noreen running off in the middle of the night?"

"Didn't she tell you?"

The three women shook their heads, giving him baleful looks as if he were somehow to blame for whatever mishap had befallen Noreen.

"She simply said we were to come watch Meg so that she could go talk to Parker. I thought she said he was at the police station," Priscilla said, "but I'd taken my hearing aid out when I went to bed and am certain I didn't hear her right."

He rolled his eyes, not appreciating Noreen leaving him with this story. The women would give him what-for, and he wasn't anticipating being looked upon as the culprit. "Someone destroyed the pumpkin field."

"Oh, no!" Hattie glanced at her sisters in consternation. "Poor Noreen!"

"Who would have done such a thing?" sweet Charlene asked in her tremulous voice.

"That's what the police are trying to figure out." Garrison's tone was grim. "They questioned me, but I'd been out."

"With Dixie, no doubt," Hattie said with great satisfaction. "You did say you'd be in late."

He sighed. "Yes, with Dixie. They called and verified my alibi with her. It seems she's more trustworthy than I am."

"Of course. She's Ned's granddaughter, and he's never steered anyone wrong." Hattie nodded, and proceeded with knitting one and purling two.

"But what about Parker?" Priscilla demanded.

"They weren't as satisfied with his whereabouts at the time the crop was vandalized."

"Well, he was here, of course!" Priscilla sounded like she couldn't believe what ninnies law officers could be. "Didn't Noreen tell them that?"

"Yes, but after he took you three home he drove around a bit. I think he'd taken a short drive along the backside of your property to look at where yours joins to Mrs. Martin's." He scratched at his head. "Anyway, I'm sure Parker will straighten them out fast enough. Plus, Noreen's due to arrive there anytime to give him moral support, so everything will work out."

Hattie pursed her lips in a grim line. She had a funny feeling Parker hadn't enjoyed being escorted off like a thief. "Why didn't Noreen go with him in the first place?"

He coughed and looked faintly ashamed. "She said they'd had words, and before the officers came to get him, she'd actually told him he'd be better off heading back to Dallas."

"Oh, dear," Charlene moaned.

"What kind of words, exactly?" Priscilla wanted to know.

Garrison's face turned a slight shade of pink in humiliation, Hattie noticed.

"I believe Parker was of the opinion that Noreen needed to stop uh, mothering me, and she was of the opinion that he ought to mind his own business," he admitted.

"Oh," all three women said in unison.

Hattie sighed. "She has carried you for quite a while, Garrison."

"I know. And I told her that Parker had a point and that she needed to get down there and tell him she'd be spending a lot more time being with him in the future than looking out for me."

The three women sat up as if electrified.

"*You* said *that?*" Hattie's tone implied that would be a miracle. Charlene and Priscilla stared, as dumbstruck as she was.

Rubbing the back of his neck, he said, "I've been a pain. But you don't have to worry about me any longer. I've reformed."

Hattie sat back in the overstuffed chair, stunned beyond words. "Well, that's one down, one to go," she muttered to herself after a moment. Of course, losing the pumpkin crop was a bigger, more heart-wrenching disaster than most, but it might still be turned to advantage... She went back to work on what looked like a small blue baby bootie, her knitting needles flashing and sparkling with silver fire. Shew! Double-whammying with her magic wand was hard work, but worth the effort if it happened....

"I'm thirsty," Cal said as Bob drove the cruiser into town. "Why don't you pull over to the Sonic and we'll get a drink. If I'm going to make it through this shift, I've gotta have a soda.''

"What about the perp?" Bob asked.

"You want something?" Cal turned to inquire of Parker.

"No, thanks," he said, sighing to himself. This was turning out to be one of the longest nights of his life. It wouldn't have been so bad if he and Noreen hadn't had irretrievable words. He wouldn't have minded so much going in for questioning then; he might have even been able to convince himself that he was pleased Rockwall's finest did their jobs so thoroughly. As it was, he was mad at Noreen, mad at himself and mad at these two lunkheads for dragging him off ignominiously in this squad car. He'd rather be driving his own car to the station, but that would have disturbed evidence, so he was stuck like this.

Noreen could have driven him, but she'd just told him to hit the road. His pride wouldn't have allowed her to drive him.

Bob pulled in between a couple of trucks, the squad car sliding into place like a well-fit shoe on a woman's foot. He turned to glance at Parker. "You sure you don't want something?"

"Are you allowed to feed the perp?" he asked smartly.

"Ah, hell, I was just kidding about that," Bob said amiably. "You're not a perp. We just have to cover all our bases."

"I know." Parker bit the inside of his jaw. "I think I'll join Cal in a soda." Heaven only knew when he'd get another chance to sit in a squad car at a Sonic drive-in.

Bob reached to punch the button on the intercom,

suddenly freezing in midair. A second later he pulled his arm back in the car and leaned over to whisper something to Cal. Carefully Cal peered past his partner at the truck next to them, where the two occupants were having a loud celebration.

Parker looked closer, instantly noticing the pumpkin parts all over the tires of the big truck. His heart began a slow hammering inside his chest.

"There's your vagrants," Bob said in a low voice.

"Procedure?" Cal inquired.

"I don't know," Bob murmured. "They sure are having a good time in there."

Parker wanted to demand that they get out and answer why there was pumpkin remains stuck in the tire treads and splashed up on the sidewalls of the truck, but he gritted his teeth and kept his mouth shut.

Bob surreptitiously leaned out the window to hear better. Raucous laughter filled the squad car. Parker squinted to see inside the cab. He could only see one of the miscreants, but that one was having a heck of a lot of fun, acting as if he were throwing something, then watching it explode. Guffaws split the air, taking Parker's temper to the boiling point.

"They haven't noticed we're here," Cal said quietly.

"Nope. Too busy partying. Stupid city boys. It just goes to show you can take the city boy to the country but you sure as heck'd be wasting your time polluting your own backyard with brainless yahoos."

"Ahem." Parker cleared his throat.

They turned to look at him, perplexed.

"I'm from Dallas," he pointed out.

"Yeah, but you're with Noreen, and that makes you a smart man," Cal explained. "Noreen wouldn't give you the time of day if you wasn't worth it, so we're giving you the benefit of the doubt.''

''I see.'' Parker leaned back, somewhat amused, yet unhappy at the same time. He'd heard about that benefit-of-the-doubt stuff before—Noreen claimed she'd give it to him the same way she'd given it to Garrison. Only she hadn't.

''Hey, Cal, why don't you get out and take a look-see over that way? They might notice me opening my door,'' Bob suggested, with a slight rolling of his eyes for Parker.

''Right.'' Cal made barely a sound getting out. He strolled nonchalantly toward the truck where the occupants were getting more fired-up by the minute. The officer made some notes, then returned to the passenger side. ''Hand me the camera.''

Bob handed it out, and Cal took a few shots before handing it back to his partner through the driver's window. Then he put beefy forearms on the passenger side of the truck and said, ''You boys sure are having a good time.''

They practically jumped out of their worthless skins, Parker noted with glee. Bob got out to meander around to the driver's side of the truck. ''You got a license I can look at?''

The occupants of the black truck were completely silent. Parker decided he wasn't a prisoner and tapped on the glass at Bob, gesturing that he wanted out. Bob opened the door with a stern expression. ''You let us handle this,'' he instructed.

''I have no intention of disturbing the fine job you two are doing,'' Parker said sincerely.

This mollified the officer, so Parker went and sat

on one of the stone benches in front of where the truck was parked.

He had never wanted to knock two heads together as badly as he did those malicious kids. Not only had they destroyed Noreen's dreams, but maybe his as well. She'd admitted wondering whether he had done it, albeit very briefly, and though he knew any sane mind would have questioned his involvement, her doubt had hurt more than he'd ever felt from Lavinia's betrayal.

He had fallen in love with Noreen. That was why his heart had felt like one of those crushed pumpkins when she'd told him to leave. He'd been fantasizing about marrying her, and the three of them living together forever.

His spirits deflated. It was time to face an irrevocable fact: she didn't feel the same way about him that he felt about her.

PARKER SAT in Noreen's kitchen, waiting for her to return. Bob and Cal had thoughtfully dropped him back home after taking the two troublemakers to the station. Those two kids had sung like birds when they'd realized they were caught with evidence, and Bob and Cal had played out their dumb cop routine admirably, getting the young men to admit that they'd been paid for the job. At that point Bob and Cal had turned a little more pointed in their questioning, getting the vandals to name their ringleader in hopes of avoiding a trip to the station.

Parker had seen red when they named Jefferson Crower as the man behind the devious deed. His emotions had sunk in the moments after, as he realized he'd brought this disaster on Noreen. If he'd never bought Widow Martin's property, Crower's rivalry might never have come to Noreen's farm. Garrison had admitted, shamefaced, to Parker that he had contacted Crower about selling his part of Cinderella Acres, only to change his mind.

Destroying the field had obviously been a guerrilla tactic to bring such financial ruin to the family that they might be forced to consider an offer from Crower.

Parker sighed, glad that the matter was in the hands of the police.

Unfortunately he had to tell Noreen, when she returned from the station. Garrison had told him that his sister had hurried off to lend him her moral and emotional support. Parker felt as small as Meg's hoppergrass. He'd accused her of hanging him out to dry to save Garrison's hide—words he desperately wished he could reclaim.

She came in the door, and his heart pounded in his chest. "Well, here I am," he said, reaching for levity.

Noreen had never been so happy to see him. "When they told me you weren't at the police station, I—" She broke off, looking at him hesitantly. The night had been such a long series of heartbreaking moments! What could she possibly say to Parker to let him know that she was sorry for the way she'd acted, the things she'd said? "I was worried," she finished lamely.

"I never really made it there." He rubbed an old spot on the wooden table aimlessly. "Only to the local Sonic."

"A lot of people go there." She rubbed her arms nervously.

"Yeah. So, apparently, did the people who ran over

your pumpkins.'' He had her full attention now. ''They were celebrating.''

''Oh. Is that what it's called,'' she said, her tone flat and unhappy. Celebrating. She had nothing to celebrate right now. She'd lost her crop and maybe Parker in the heat of moment.

''I think they'd poured a good bit of whisky into their cups.'' Running a hand through his hair, he shot her a tentative glance. ''Jefferson Crower put them up to sabotaging you.''

Parker's business rival. She might have known. ''Retaliation?''

He shrugged. ''Maybe. Very likely he was trying to outdo me, but it didn't help that Garrison had called to discuss selling his acreage. Although he backed out,'' he said hastily. ''Noreen, I'm sorry. Whether I intended it or not, you did become an instrument of revenge. Since I got you into this, I wish you'd let me help get you out of it.''

''I don't know what to say.'' So many forces had combined to make her doubt Parker. They'd been on opposite sides from the start. Yet they had so much to give each other. ''Yes, I do know what to say. I wish I hadn't told you to go back to Dallas.'' She could feel tears pressing at the back of her eyes. Nerves, she told herself, for losing her crop—but it was so much more than that. ''I should know better than to speak when I'm upset, and I felt torn between my loyalties.'' She looked at him, feeling as if her words were inadequate. ''Could you forgive me, and allow me to rescind my request for you to leave the premises? It's one of my most fervent wishes.''

He got up and crossed the room to look down into her eyes. ''That wish is easily granted.''

She put her hands out to him, and he pulled her to him, stroking her back. "Noreen, you've been through a lot. I'm just glad you're still speaking to me."

"I have to," she whispered, looking up at him. "I've fallen in love with you."

"You have?" His chest tightened around the area of his heart.

"I'm afraid so. Anything I've said to the contrary was simply…insecurity talking."

He kissed the tip of her nose. "You're not insecure about anything."

"I am about handsome princes sweeping me off my feet."

"I see." He kissed her lips lightly. "Well, I'm not a prince. I'm just a regular guy who's completely in love with you."

"I hope so, Parker," she whispered.

"I asked you to marry me, didn't I? And I know you wanted to think it was only for Meg's sake, but don't sell yourself short, lady. I'd be less than a prince to let you get away from me."

"Oh, Parker," she murmured. "You and your fairy tales."

"If I have to try on every boot in the city to prove to you that I fit out here with you, then I'll do it."

His voice was a soft rasp against her hair. Noreen closed her eyes as she leaned against his chest. He was a dream man. Aunt Hattie had done such a good job with her scheming. This time, she'd have it all: Parker and his wonderful princess of a daughter who wanted jeans and grasshoppers, a trio of lovable relatives and her beloved Cinderella Acres.

"Never mind the boots," she whispered. "I'll settle for trying a wedding band on you."

"You will?" Parker waited to see the answer in her eyes before he kissed her, long and slowly. Noreen sighed as the sweet emotions swept over her.

"Yes. I've always wanted to live happily ever after."

He swept her up into his arms. "Let's get started."

"Are you taking me to Meg's room so we can tell her?"

"I am, indeed."

She snuggled against his chest. "I can only hope she'll be as happy about me as she was about Meanie and hunting arrowheads."

"She'll be more than happy." He enfolded her in his arms. "I have something I must tell you."

"Not another story," she said with a mischievous grin.

He chuckled. "No, this is real-life true. I didn't outbid Crower for Mrs. Martin's property, but I didn't know that until after we'd signed the papers." He leaned back to grin at her. "Apparently, my money wasn't the enticing factor any more than it has been with you."

She gave him a playful tap on the lips. "Of course not. Mr. and Mrs. Martin were happily married for many years because their only priority was each other. But why did she sell to you?"

"When she and her husband got married, they bought that farm with the only money they had. I had told her I wanted to buy it to give to you for a wedding present, and she said that she was going to sell it to me because her husband would have liked the idea of another young married couple owning it.

Starting out together, working with the same goals in mind.''

''So that was your big secret.''

''The only one I've kept from you. I promise you that.''

Her eyes glowed with happiness, but she felt like she had to give him one last chance to understand what he was getting himself into. ''It's a lot of land combined with mine. There'll be long days involved.''

''Then I'd better get rested up now,'' he whispered as they crossed the upstairs threshold, ''because I plan on loving your boots off at night.''

Epilogue

Six months later

"What if she doesn't take him?"

Priscilla spoke the question aloud that was on everyone's mind. Charlene and Hattie frowned. Noreen, three months pregnant now, glanced at Parker worriedly. His mouth turned down as he patted her back soothingly. Meg's little dark eyebrows rose as she looked around the parlor at her family before she went back to playing on the oval rug with her arrowhead collection. Ned cracked his knuckles loudly. They all jumped when the mantel clock chimed.

Garrison had been gone two hours. He'd gone to ask Dixie to marry him, because today was the end of their six-month agreement to date each other. Today she would either say "Yes," or "Deal's off," as they'd agreed.

Ned had a lot riding on the answer Garrison brought home. Hattie wouldn't marry him until both of her charges were safely married off, she'd vowed. He rubbed his chin glumly. The limo business he and Garrison had started with one limo, and for which Parker served as consultant, had started off with a bang. It was doing so well, in fact, that if Garrison managed to pull a yes out of Dixie, Ned planned on talking to his future son-in-law about adding one more limo to the small fleet of taxis they had. Then he was taking Hattie on a heckuva honeymoon in one of those long, shiny limos.

If she said yes.

Noreen and Parker hoped Dixie would accept Garrison. They intended to ask them to be their new baby's godparents. Noreen sighed, and Parker put his hand over hers.

I shouldn't ask for more happiness, she told herself. There had been so much since Parker and Meg had come into her life! Parker was good to her, and Noreen loved Meg with all her heart. The three of them enjoyed bringing Cinderella Acres back to the beauty and profitability the farm deserved. Because she wouldn't allow Parker to help her financially, he'd come up with a different slant on the fairy tale. The day before their wedding Noreen had looked out the kitchen window, and there was Parker and Meg bringing home a brand new air-conditioned tractor. Her coach, Parker had called it.

She smiled, remembering how thrilled she'd been with his gift. But it was her new family that brought her the most happiness. Putting one hand to her stomach, she fervently wished for the same happiness for Garrison. He deserved it, too! She couldn't really have a happy ending until he did. It had meant so much to their father that they be close. He'd wanted them to stick together like a real family. It had been rocky for her and Garrison, but a startling change had been wrought in his life—and hers. Now the final icing of love and contentment was just within his grasp.

If Dixie will just say yes.

Suddenly, barking interrupted the silence. They all jumped to their feet to stare out the parlor window. A black-and-white collie bounded up the lane toward the house wearing a huge red bow around his neck.

Meg clapped her hands. "A doggie!"

"It is a doggie," Noreen murmured. "Let's go see who it belongs to."

"Looks like Dixie's," Ned said. "But that couldn't be possible."

They all filed out onto the porch. The dog sat down for them, his tongue licking at their hands.

"There's a piece of paper on his collar!" Noreen bent to retrieve it. Opening it, she read aloud, "'My name is Rascal. Can you keep me for a week? Garrison and Dixie are flying to Bermuda for a honeymoon and say you'll take very good care of me.'"

"Oh, my stars!" Hattie clapped her hands. Ned grabbed her for a delighted hug.

Noreen and Parker picked Meg up together in a three-way family hug. "I think that's a yes," Noreen said as she kissed her husband.

At the end of the lane a motorcycle appeared. Rascal bounded off to greet his mistress and her fiancé, who appeared to be hanging on successfully for the ride.

Charlene and Priscilla smiled at each other. They nodded Hattie's way. "Guess her magic wand is still capable of a trick or two," Priscilla said.

"Mighty powerful to pull off such a miracle," Charlene agreed.

"We might have to go easier on her in the future,"

Priscilla murmured, watching happily as Ned kissed Hattie right on her little button mouth. "She knew what she was doing all along."

"Not *too* easy," Charlene said. "Without her small disasters, we'd have nothing at all to be grateful for!"

AFTERWARD, when Meg was tucked in her bed with an adoring Rascal sleeping on top of her covers, Parker and Noreen went for a long, slow walk in the sultry evening shadows. Noreen sighed with sheer happiness, and Parker pulled her close as they walked through the pumpkin field.

"I love you," he said.

"I love you, too," she replied. "And it all worked out, didn't it?"

He drew her to him for a lingering kiss. "Yes. It has."

"I worried about us all fitting together, but it's a dream come true. And our baby's going to be so lucky to have Meg for a big sister." She gave herself up to his embrace. "You know, you may not be single anymore, but you sure are a sexy dad."

"And you," Parker said with a glow in his eyes, "are one red-hot mama."

"I'm not!" she said, laughing.

"You are." He ran one hand along her waist and cupped her head with the other. "If you have time, I can show you how certain I am of that fact."

She lifted her lips for another sweet kiss as the sky softened over Cinderella Acres. "I can stay out past midnight, my love, and then some."

"Good," he whispered, "because I'll be under your spell for the rest of my life."

Noreen smiled to herself as Parker gently claimed

her lips. There was no magic spell, of course. Finding her prince and his precious daughter was a real-life miracle, a happy ending they'd treasure for the rest of their lives.

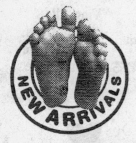

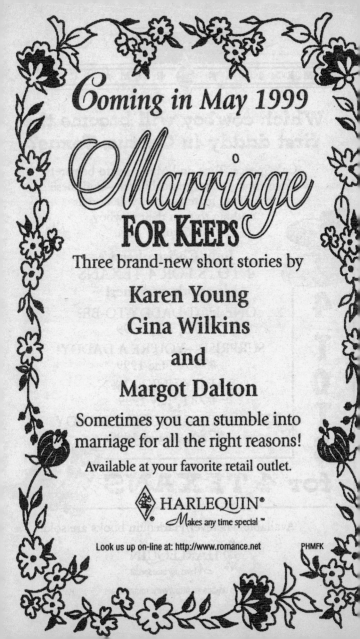

COMING NEXT MONTH

#773 ONE HOT DADDY-TO-BE? by Judy Christenberry
4 Tots for 4 Texans
Nothing is more important for four elderly mothers of Cactus, Texas,
than making their sons fathers. They're not even above a little bet...so
the baby race is on! Bachelor #1, Cal Baxter, never knew he'd one day be
looking at his childhood friend Jessica Hoya as a prospective mother of
his child...but he never knew how determined his mother could be!

#774 THE LAST TWO BACHELORS by Linda Randall Wisdom
Delaney's Grooms
"You've just seen your new mother." The prophetic note that ring
bearer Patric pulls out of his tux pocket tells him he and his dad,
Jack O'Connor, have a prospect for a new wife and mom...but how could
that be, when she's the beautiful woman trying on a wedding gown?

#775 THE ACCIDENTAL MRS. MacKENZIE by Bonnie K. Winn
Brynn Magee had imagined herself to be Douglas MacKenzie's bride for
months. But when his family suddenly mistakes her for his real-life bride,
she realizes she's in love with Matt MacKenzie—the "groom's" brother!

#776 FATHER IN TRAINING by Mollie Molay
New Arrivals
It was one of those things: a moonlit night, an incredibly sexy guy,
music in the background. Before she knew what happened, Abby Carson
was in the arms of the man she'd been wishing for all her life. But now,
was Jeff Logan ready to be a daddy?

Look us up on-line at: http://www.romance.net